IRÈNE NÉMIROVSKY

Le Bal

and

Snow in Autumn

Translated from the French by Sandra Smith

VINTAGE BOOKS
London

Published by Vintage 2007

2 4 6 8 10 9 7 5 3 1

Copyright © Éditions Bernard Grasset, 1930 (*Le Bal*) and 1931
(*Snow in Autumn*)
Translation copyright © Sandra Smith, 2007

Licence arranged by the French Publishers' Agency in New York

Irène Némirovsky has asserted her right under the Copyright, Designs
and Patents Act 1988 to be identified as the author of this work

Le Bal was first published in France by Éditions Bernard Grasset in 1930
Snow in Autumn was first published in France as *Les Mouches d'automne*
by Éditions Bernard Grasset in 1931

First published in Great Britain in 2007 by Vintage

Vintage
Random House, 20 Vauxhall Bridge Road,
London SW1V 2SA

www.vintage-books.co.uk

Addresses for companies within
The Random House Group Limited can be found at:
www.randomhouse.co.uk/offices.htm

The Random House Group Limited Reg. No. 954009

A CIP catalogue record for this book
is available from the British Library

ISBN 9780099493976

The Random House Group Limited makes every effort to ensure
that the papers used in its books are made from trees that have been
legally sourced from well-managed and credibly certified forests.
Our paper procurement policy can be found at:
www.randomhouse.co.uk/paper.htm

Mixed Sources
Product group from well-managed
forests and other controlled sources
www.fsc.org Cert no. TT-COC-2139
© 1996 Forest Stewardship Council
FSC

Typeset by Palimpsest Book Production Limited,
Grangemouth, Stirlingshire

Printed and bound in Great Britain by
CPI Bookmarque, Croydon CR0 4TD

LE BAL

Irène Némirovsky was born in Kiev in 1903, the daughter of a successful Jewish banker. In 1918 her family fled the Russian Revolution for France where she became a bestselling novelist, author of *David Golder* and other works published in her lifetime, as well as the posthumous *Suite Française* and *Chaleur du Sang* (*Fire in the Blood*). Prevented from publishing when the Germans occupied France in 1940, she moved with her husband and two small daughters from Paris to the safety of the small village of Issy-l'Evêque (in German occupied territory). It was here that Irène began writing *Suite Française*, published to wide acclaim in 2005. She died in Auschwitz in 1942.

ALSO BY IRÈNE NÉMIROVSKY

David Golder
Suite Française
Fire in the Blood

Translator's Preface

Since the publication of *Suite Française*, many of Irène Némirovsky's earlier works are being reprinted in French and translated into many languages. The two novellas in this volume, *Le Bal* and *Snow in Autumn*, show the author at her most skilful, mastering the genre to present an insightful analysis of two of her most important themes: the interaction between different members of a family and how foreigners were treated in the Parisian society of the 1930s.

In *Le Bal*, written in 1930, Némirovsky presents the Kampf family. Alfred, a German Jewish immigrant, struggles to be accepted for years until he makes a fortune on the Stock Market. Once wealthy, he marries Rosine, a woman with a dubious moral background, and converts to Catholicism for her. They have a daughter, Antoinette, whose relationship with her mother is complex and hostile. Rosine is obsessed with being accepted into the upper classes, material possessions and status. The ball they give is intended to confirm their acceptance in Parisian high society, but Rosine's and Antoinette's relationship will intervene to give the tale a scathing twist.

With *Snow in Autumn* Irène Némirovsky gives us her unique perspective into Russian society in the process of collapse, during the Revolution of 1917, and the effect on the White Russians: the fortunate ones who survived, who were stripped of all their possessions and forced into exile.

The story follows the experiences of the Karine family, wealthy White Russians, told from the perspective of their faithful old nanny, Tatiana Ivanovna. Némirovsky skilfully details the plight of many such families of the time who, having lost everything, immigrate to Paris. Their fear, poverty and desperate attempts to make a new life in a strange country, where foreigners were treated with suspicion and contempt, are sensitively treated by Némirovsky. *Snow in Autumn* is a moving tale that is unforgettable.

Sandra Smith
Robinson College
Cambridge
August 2007

Le Bal

1

Madame Kampf walked into the study and slammed the door behind her with such force that a gust of air made the crystal beads on the chandelier jingle with the pure, light sound of small bells. But Antoinette didn't stop reading; she was bent so far forward over her desk that her hair brushed the pages of her book. For a moment, Madame Kampf watched her daughter without saying anything; then she went to stand in front of her, arms crossed over her chest.

'You know, Antoinette, you could stop what you're doing when you see your mother,' she barked. 'Is your bottom glued to that chair? What refined manners you have! Where's Miss Betty?'

From the adjoining room came the sound of a sewing machine, punctuated by snatches of song, crooned in a youthful but rather poor voice: 'What shall I do, what shall I do when you'll be gone away . . .'

'Miss Betty,' Madame Kampf shouted, 'come in here.'

'Yes, Mrs Kampf,' the young woman replied in English, slipping through the half-open door. She had rosy cheeks and soft, frightened eyes; her hair was gathered in a honey-coloured bun that sat low on her neck, framing her small round head.

'I believe I hired you,' Madame Kampf began harshly, 'to look after and educate my daughter, and not so you could make yourself dresses. Does Antoinette not know she is

3

meant to stand up when her mother comes into the room?'

'Oh, Ann-toinette! How can you?' said Miss Betty in a kind of sad twitter.

Antoinette was standing up now, balancing awkwardly on one leg. She was a tall, lacklustre girl of fourteen, with the pale face common to girls of her age – a face so thin and taut that it seems, to adults, like a round, featureless blotch. Dark circles were under her lowered eyelids, and her mouth was small and tight. The fourteen-year-old body . . . budding breasts that strain against the tight schoolgirl's uniform, that are painful and embarrassing to her delicate, childlike body; big feet and long arms like sticks of French bread that end in red hands and ink-stained fingers (and which one day, who knows, might turn into the most beautiful arms in the world); a spindly neck; short, dull hair that is dry and fine . . .

'Don't you see, Antoinette, that your manners are driving me to despair? Sit down again. I'm going to come back in, and this time you will do me the honour of standing up immediately, understand?'

Madame Kampf took a few steps out of the room and once again opened the door. Antoinette stood up so slowly and with such obvious reluctance that her mother clenched her teeth.

'Perhaps you can't be bothered, is that it, Miss?' she asked sharply, her voice threatening.

'No, Mama,' replied Antoinette quietly.

'Well, then why have you got that look on your face?'

Antoinette attempted a smile, but with so little effort that it merely distorted her features into an unfortunate grimace. Sometimes she hated grown-ups so much that she could have killed them, mutilated them, or at least stamped her foot and shouted, 'No! Just leave me alone!' But her parents frightened her. Ever since she was a tiny child, she'd been afraid of her parents.

When Antoinette was small, her mother had often held her on her lap, cuddled her, and kissed her. But Antoinette had forgotten all that. Instead she remembered what it was like to hear the roar of an angry voice above her head: 'You're always under my feet, Antoinette . . .'; 'Don't tell me you've dirtied my dress with your filthy shoes again! Go and stand in the corner, do you hear me? That will teach you, you little idiot!'; and one day on a street corner – the day when, for the first time, she had wanted to die – a shout so loud, during one of their scenes, that passers-by had turned round to stare: 'Do you want me to smack you? Do you?' Deep in her heart she remembered how that slap burned her face. Right in the middle of the street! She had been eleven then, but big for her age. The passers-by, the grown-ups, she didn't care about them . . . But some boys had been coming out of school, and they'd laughed when they'd seen her: 'Oh you poor thing!' Their sniggering had followed her as she walked, head down, along the dark autumn avenue, the street-lamps a blur through her tears. 'Haven't you finished snivelling yet? You've got no character! You must know I punish you for your own good! And I'm warning you . . . You'd better not annoy me again, or else.' People were horrible . . . And, even now, she was hounded from morning to night, as if deliberately to torment her, torture her, humiliate her: 'Look at how you're holding your fork!' (in front of the servants, for God's sake); and 'Stand up straight. Or at least try not to look like a hunchback.' She was fourteen years old, a young lady – and, in her dreams, a woman who was beautiful, adored . . . She turned men's heads. They caressed her the way Andrea Sperelli caressed Elena and Maria in D'Annunzio's *Il Piacere*, the way Julien de Suberceaux caressed Maud de Rouvre. Love . . . She trembled at the thought of it.

'And if you think that I'm paying an English governess so you can have manners like that, you are very much mistaken, young lady!'

Madame Kampf lowered her voice.

'You keep forgetting that we're rich now, Antoinette,' she said, pushing back a lock of hair that had fallen on to her daughter's face.

She turned to the Englishwoman.

'I have a lot of errands for you to run this week, Miss Betty. I'm holding a ball on the fifteenth . . .'

'A ball,' murmured Antoinette, her eyes opening wide.

'Yes,' said Madame Kampf, smiling, 'a ball . . .'

She looked at Antoinette with pride, then frowned, indicating the Englishwoman with a slight twitch of the eyebrow.

'I don't suppose you've been talking, have you?'

'No, Mama, no,' Antoinette quickly replied.

She knew all too well her mother's constant worry. At first – two years ago now, in 1926, when they'd left the Rue Favart after her father had made a killing on the Stock Market (first on the devaluation of the franc and then of the pound) and they'd become rich – Antoinette had been called into her parents' bedroom every morning. Her mother would be lying in bed polishing her nails; in the adjoining dressing room, her father, a dry little Jew with fiery eyes, would be shaving, washing, and getting dressed, all with the same breakneck speed that characterised his every action and which, in the past, had earned him the nickname 'Feuer' amongst the German Jews, his friends at the Stock Market. For years Alfred Kampf had haunted the great steps of the Stock Market without getting anywhere. Antoinette knew that he used to be an employee of the Banque de Paris and, long before that, a doorman at the bank, wearing a blue uniform. Shortly before Antoinette was born, he'd married his mistress, Mademoiselle Rosine, the manager's secretary. For eleven years they had lived in a small, dingy apartment behind the Opéra Comique. Antoinette remembered how the maid would crash about in the kitchen washing the dishes while she sat at the dining-room table doing her homework, Madame Kampf reading novels beside her, leaning forward to catch the light from the large gas-lamp with the round frosted glass shade that hung above them. Now and again Madame Kampf would let out an angry sigh so loud and sudden that it made Antoinette jump. 'What is it now?' Kampf would ask. And Rosine would reply, 'It makes me feel sick when I think of how some people have such an easy life, how happy they are, while I'm stuck here, in this dirty hole, spending the best years of my life darning your socks . . .'

Kampf would simply shrug without saying anything. At this point Rosine would usually look at Antoinette and shout bad-temperedly, 'And why are *you* listening? Is it any of your business what grown-ups are talking about?' rounding off the reprimand with, 'Yes, that's it, girl. If you're waiting for your father to make his fortune like he's been promising to ever since we got married, you'll be waiting a very long time, you'll watch your whole life slip by . . . You'll grow up, and you'll still be here, like your poor mother, waiting . . .' When she said the word 'waiting', a certain look came over her tense, sullen features, an expression so pathetic, so deeply pained, that Antoinette was often moved, in spite of herself, to lean forward and kiss her mother on the cheek.

'My poor baby,' Rosine would then say, stroking her daughter's face. But once she had shouted, 'Oh, leave me alone won't you! You're annoying me. You can be so irritating! Yes, you as well . . .' And never again had Antoinette given her mother a kiss, except in the morning and at night – the kind of kiss parents and children give each other automatically, like two strangers shaking hands.

Then, one fine day, they had suddenly become rich. Antoinette had never understood how. They had come to live in a vast white apartment, and her mother had suddenly appeared with her hair dyed blonde. Antoinette had glanced furtively, fearfully, at the flaming gold tresses which she hardly recognised.

'So tell me again, Antoinette,' Madame Kampf would order from her bed each morning, 'what do you answer if someone asks you where we lived last year?'

'You're an idiot,' Kampf would say from the dressing room. 'Who do you think is going to talk to her? She doesn't know anyone.'

'I know what I'm talking about,' Madame Kampf replied, raising her voice. 'What about the servants?'

'If I catch her saying a single word to the servants, she'll have me to deal with,' said Kampf, coming into the bedroom. 'You understand, Antoinette? She knows she just has to keep her mouth shut and learn her lessons, and that's the end of it. We ask nothing more of her ...' Turning to his wife, Kampf added, 'She's not a fool, you know.'

But as soon as he had left, Madame Kampf started in again.

'If anyone asks you, Antoinette, you're to say we lived in the Midi all last year. You don't need to go into detail as to whether it was in Cannes or Nice, just say the Midi ... unless they ask for details, in which case it would be better to say Cannes, it's more sophisticated ... But, of course, your father is right, it's best to say nothing at all. A little girl should speak as little as possible to grown-ups.'

And she sent her away with a wave of her beautiful bare arm, a slightly thick arm, sparkling with the diamond bracelet her husband had just given her and which she only ever took off in the bath.

Antoinette was remembering all this when she heard her mother ask the Englishwoman, 'Does Antoinette at least have nice handwriting?'

'Yes, Mrs Kampf.'

'Why?' Antoinette asked shyly.

'Because,' explained Madame Kampf, 'you can help me

8

write out the envelopes this evening. You see, I'm sending nearly two hundred invitations. I'll never manage it alone ... Miss Betty, I'm giving Antoinette permission to go to bed an hour later than usual tonight. You'd like that, wouldn't you?' she asked, turning towards her daughter.

But as Antoinette was once again lost in thought and said nothing, Madame Kampf shrugged her shoulders.

'That girl has always got her head in the clouds,' she remarked quietly. 'Doesn't it make you proud to think your parents are giving a ball?' she asked her daughter. 'Well, doesn't it? I fear you don't have much feeling, my poor girl,' she concluded with a sigh, as she turned and left the room.

2

Antoinette was usually put to bed by the English governess at nine o'clock precisely, but that evening, she stayed in the drawing room with her parents. She was so rarely allowed in there that she stared at the white panelling and gilt furniture as if she were visiting someone else's house. Her mother pointed to a small pedestal table laid out with ink, pens, and a packet of cards with envelopes.

'Sit down over there. I'll dictate the addresses to you,' she said, then turned to her husband and asked loudly, 'Will you be joining us, my dear?' The servant was clearing away the dishes in the adjoining room, and for several months now, the Kampfs had made a point of addressing each other with great formality in front of him. But as soon as Kampf got close enough, Rosine whispered, 'For heaven's sake, get rid of that flunkey, will you. He's so annoying . . .'

She noticed the look on Antoinette's face and blushed.

'Will you be much longer, Georges?' she asked imperiously. 'You may go as soon as you've finished putting those things away.'

The three of them then sat in silence, frozen to their chairs. When the servant had gone, Madame Kampf let out a sigh.

'I can't stand that Georges, I don't know why. As soon as I sense him behind me at dinner, I lose my appetite . . . And just what are you smirking about, Antoinette? Come on, let's get to work. Do you have the guest list, Alfred?'

10

'Yes,' replied Kampf, 'but first let me take off my jacket. I'm hot.'

'Just make sure that you remember not to leave it lying around in here like the last time,' said his wife. 'I could tell from the looks on their faces that Georges and Lucie found it odd that you were in the drawing room in your shirtsleeves . . .'

'I don't give a damn about the opinions of the servants,' Kampf grumbled.

'Well, you're very wrong, my dear. It's the servants who make or break reputations, going from one place to another and talking . . . I would have never known that the baroness on the third floor . . .'

She lowered her voice and whispered something that Antoinette, despite all her efforts, failed to hear.

'. . . without Lucie who was with her for three years . . .'

Kampf reached into his pocket and pulled out a piece of paper covered with names, many of which were crossed out.

'Let's start with the people I know, all right, Rosine? Antoinette, you write. Monsieur and Madame Banyuls. I don't know their address, but you have the telephone directory there, so you can look up any addresses we need . . .'

'They're extremely rich, aren't they?' Rosine murmured with respect.

'Extremely.'

'Do you think they'll want to come? I don't know Madame Banyuls.'

'Neither do I. But I do business with her husband, so that's sufficient . . . I've heard his wife is charming, and besides, she doesn't receive many invitations from his circle since she was mixed up in that business . . . you know, the famous orgies in the Bois de Boulogne, two years ago . . .'

'Alfred, not in front of the child!'

'She doesn't understand. You just write, Antoinette . . . Nevertheless, she's a good person to start with . . .'

11

'Don't forget the Ostiers,' Rosine said quickly. 'It seems they give wonderful parties . . .'

'Monsieur and Madame Ostier d'Arrachon, number two . . . Antoinette . . . Well, my dear, I don't know about them. They're very prim and proper, very . . . The wife used to be . . .'

He made a gesture.

'No!'

'Yes. I know someone who used to see her in a brothel in Marseille . . . Yes, yes, I can assure you . . . But that was a long time ago, nearly twenty years. Her marriage completely transformed her. Now she receives very classy people, and she's extremely particular when it comes to her friends. As a general rule, all women with a past get like that after ten years.'

'My God,' sighed Madame Kampf, 'it's so difficult . . .'

'We must be methodical, my dear. For a first party, invite anyone and everyone – as many of the sods as you can stand. When it comes to the second or third you can start to be selective. This time, we have to invite everyone in sight.'

'But if we could at least be sure that everyone would come . . . If anyone refused, I think I'd die of shame . . .'

Kampf grimaced and stifled a laugh.

'If anyone refuses to come, then you'll invite them again the next time, and again the time after that. What do you want me to say? In the end, if you want to get ahead in society, you simply have to obey the Gospels religiously.'

'What on earth do you mean?'

'If someone slaps you, turn the other cheek . . . Society is the best school in which to learn Christian humility.'

'I do wonder,' said Madame Kampf, somewhat shocked, 'where you get all these stupid ideas, my dear.'

Kampf smiled.

'Come on then, let's get on with it . . . Here's a piece of

paper with some addresses on it. All you have to do is copy them, Antoinette . . .'

Madame Kampf leaned over her daughter's shoulder as she continued writing, her head lowered.

'It's true she has very nice handwriting, very neat . . . Tell me, Alfred, Monsieur Julien Nassan . . . Wasn't he the one who was in prison for fraud?'

'Nassan? Yes.'

'Oh!' murmured Rosine, rather surprised.

'But why that look?' asked Kampf. 'He's recovered his position, he's a charming young man, and a first-class businessman what's more . . .'

'Monsieur Julien Nassan, 23A Avenue Hoche,' Antoinette read out. 'Who's next, Papa?'

'There are only twenty-five more,' Madame Kampf groaned. 'We'll never find two hundred people, Alfred!'

'Of course we will. Come now, don't start getting all upset. Where's your own list? All the people you met in Nice, Deauville, Chamonix last year . . .'

Madame Kampf took a notepad from the table.

'Count Moïssi, Monsieur and Madame Lévy de Brunelleschi and the Marquis d'Itcharra: he's Madame Lévy's lover; they're always invited everywhere together . . .'

'Is there a husband, at least?' asked Kampf doubtfully.

'I understand that they are very respectable people. There are some more marquises, you know, five of them. The Marquis de Liguès y Hermosa, the Marquis . . . Tell me, Alfred, are we supposed to use their titles when we speak to them? I think we should, don't you? Not *Monsieur le Marquis* like the servants, of course, but *my dear Marquis, my dear Countess* . . . If we don't, the others won't even notice we're receiving the aristocracy.'

'Maybe you'd like it if we pinned labels to their backs, eh?'

'Oh, you and your idiotic jokes! Come on, Antoinette, hurry up and copy those out, darling . . .'

Antoinette wrote for a moment, then read out loud: 'The Baron and Baroness Levinstein-Lévy, the Count and Countess Poirier . . .'

'That's Abraham and Rebecca Birnbaum. They bought that title. Don't you think it's idiotic to call yourself Poirier, like a tree? If it was up to me, I'd choose . . .'

She drifted off into a deep dream.

'Just *Count and Countess Kampf*,' she murmured. 'That doesn't sound bad at all.'

'Wait a while,' Kampf suggested. 'We've got at least ten years before that . . .'

Rosine was sorting through some visiting cards that had been thrown into a malachite bowl decorated with gilt Chinese dragons.

'Still, I'd really like to know who all these people are,' she mused. 'There's a whole batch of cards here I got at New Year . . . Loads from all those little gigolos I met in Deauville . . .'

'We need as many people as possible to fill the gaps. So long as they're dressed correctly . . .'

'Oh, my dear, you are joking. At least they're all counts, marquises, viscounts . . . But I can't seem to match their faces to their names . . . They all look alike. Still, it doesn't really matter, in the end. You saw how it was done at the Rothwan de Fiesques' party? You say exactly the same thing to everyone: "So *pleased* to see you . . ." and then, if you're forced to introduce two people, you just mumble. No one can ever hear anything . . . Come on, Antoinette, darling, what you're doing isn't hard. The addresses are on the cards . . .'

'But, Mama,' Antoinette interrupted, 'this one's the upholsterer's card . . .'

'What are you talking about? Let me see. Good God, she's right. I'm going out of my mind, Alfred, I really am . . . How many is that, Antoinette?'

'One hundred and seventy-two, Mama.'

'Well, that's not so bad!'

The Kampfs sighed with satisfaction and smiled at each other with the same expression of weary triumph as two actors after the third curtain call.

'We're doing well, aren't we?'

'Mademoiselle Isabelle Cossette . . . That's . . . that's not *my* Mademoiselle Isabelle, is it?' Antoinette asked shyly.

'But of course . . .'

'But why are you inviting her?' exclaimed Antoinette, then blushed violently, expecting a curt 'What business is it of yours?' from her mother. But Madame Kampf seemed awkward.

'She's a fine young woman . . . We have to be nice to people . . .'

'She's absolutely ghastly,' Antoinette protested.

Mademoiselle Isabelle, a cousin of the Kampfs, was music teacher to several families of rich Jewish stockbrokers. She was a boring old maid, as stiff and upright as an umbrella; she taught Antoinette piano and music theory. Extremely short-sighted but refusing to wear glasses because she was proud of her rather pretty eyes and thick eyelashes, she would lean over the piano and glue her big pointed nose, bluish from rice powder, to the music. Whenever Antoinette made a mistake, she would hit her fingers sharply with an ebony ruler that was as hard and flat as she was. She was as malicious and prying as a magpie. The night before her music lessons, Antoinette would whisper a fervent prayer (her father had converted when he got married; Antoinette had been raised a Catholic): 'Please God, let Mademoiselle Isabelle die tonight.'

'The child's right,' Kampf remarked in surprise. 'What's got into you to make you want to invite that old madwoman? You can't actually like her . . .'

Madame Kampf shrugged her shoulders angrily.

'Oh, you don't understand anything! How do you expect my family to hear about it otherwise? Can't you just picture the look on their faces? Aunt Loridon, who fell out with me because I married a Jew, and Julie Lacombe and Uncle Martial, and everyone in the family who looked down their noses at us because they had more money than us, remember? It's very simple: if we don't invite Isabelle, I can't be sure that the next day they'll all die of envy, and then it's not worth having the ball at all! Keep writing, Antoinette.'

'Shall we have dancing in both reception rooms?'

'Of course, and in our hall . . . It's very beautiful, our hall . . . I'll hire great baskets of flowers. Just wait till you see how wonderful it will look filled with beautiful women in their most elegant dresses and best jewellery, the men in evening dress . . . It looked positively magical at the Lévy de Brunelleschis'. During the tangos, they switched off the electricity and left on two large alabaster lamps in the corners of the room that gave off a red light . . .'

'I don't care much for that idea. Makes it look like a dance hall . . .'

'But everyone seems to be doing it now. Women love letting men have a little feel to the music . . . The supper, naturally, on small tables . . .'

'How about having a bar to start off with?'

'That's a good idea . . . We need to warm them up when they arrive. We could set up the bar in Antoinette's room. She can sleep in the linen room or in the boxroom at the end of the corridor just for one night . . .'

Antoinette went pale and started trembling violently.

'Couldn't I stay for just a quarter of an hour?' she whispered, her words almost choking her.

A ball . . . My God, was it possible that there could take place – here, right under her nose – this splendid thing she vaguely imagined as a mixture of wild music, intoxicating perfumes, dazzling evening gowns, words of love whispered

16

in some isolated alcove, as dark and cool as a hidden chamber
. . . and that she could be sent to bed that night, like any
other night, at nine o'clock, like a baby? Perhaps the men
who knew the Kampfs had a daughter would ask where she
was – and her mother would answer with her hateful little
laugh, 'Oh, but really, she's been asleep for hours . . .' And
yet what harm would it do to her if Antoinette, yes Antoinette
as well, had a bit of happiness in this life? My God, to be
able to dance, just once, wearing a pretty dress, like a real
young lady, held tightly in a man's arms! She closed her eyes
and repeated, 'Just a quarter of an hour, can't I, Mama?'
with a kind of bold despair, as if she were pointing a loaded
revolver at her heart.

'What?' shouted Madame Kampf, stunned. 'Don't you
dare ask again . . .'

'You'll go to Monsieur Blanc's ball,' said her father.

Madame Kampf shrugged her shoulders.

'I think this child must be mad . . .'

Antoinette's face suddenly contorted.

'Please, Mama, please, I'm begging you!' she shouted. 'I'm
fourteen, Mama, I'm not a little girl any more. I *know* girls
come out at fifteen, but I look fifteen, and next year . . .'

Madame Kampf exploded.

'Well, honestly, how wonderful! Honestly!' she shouted,
her voice hoarse with anger. 'This kid, this snotty-nosed kid,
coming to the ball! Can you just picture it? Just you wait,
girl, I'll knock all those fancy ideas right out of you. You
think you're going to "come out" next year, eh? Who's been
putting ideas like that in your head? You listen to me. I've
only just begun to live, *me*, you hear, *me*, and I have no
intention of rushing to lumber myself with having to marry
off a daughter . . . I don't know why I shouldn't box your
ears to teach you a lesson,' she continued in the same tone
of voice, while walking towards Antoinette.

Antoinette stepped back and went even whiter. The lost,

desperate expression in her eyes caused Kampf to feel a kind of pity.

'Come on now, leave her be,' he said, catching Rosine's raised arm. 'The child's tired and upset, she doesn't know what she's saying . . . Go to bed, Antoinette.'

Antoinette didn't move; her mother shoved her by the shoulders.

'Go on, out, and not a word. Move it, or I'm warning you . . .'

Antoinette was shaking from head to foot, but she walked slowly out of the room holding back her tears.

'Charming,' said Madame Kampf after she'd gone. 'That girl's going to be a handful . . . I was just the same at her age, though. But I'm not like my poor mother who never knew how to say no to me . . . I'll keep her in her place, I promise you that . . .'

'She'll calm down when she's had some sleep. She was tired. It's eleven o'clock already; she's not used to going to bed so late. That's why she got upset . . . Let's carry on with the list,' said Kampf, 'and forget about it.'

3

In the middle of the night, Miss Betty was woken by the sound of sobbing in the next room. She switched on the light and listened for a moment through the wall. It was the first time she had heard the girl cry: usually when Madame Kampf scolded her, Antoinette managed to hold back her tears and say nothing.

'*What's the matter with you, child? Are you ill?*' she called through the wall.

The sobbing stopped.

'I suppose your mother scolded you. It's for your own good, you know, Antoinette . . . Tomorrow you'll apologise to her, you'll give each other a kiss, and it will be all over. It's late now, you should get some sleep. Would you like some herbal tea? No? You could answer me, you know, my dearest,' she said, as Antoinette remained silent. '*Dear, dear*, a little girl sulking isn't a pretty sight. You're upsetting your guardian angel . . .'

Antoinette made a face and stretched out her clenched little fists towards the wall. Bloody woman. Bloody selfish hypocrites, the lot of them . . . They couldn't care less that she was crying all alone in the dark, so hard she could barely breathe . . . that she felt as miserable and lonely as a lost dog!

No one loved her, no one in the whole world . . . But couldn't they see, blind idiots, that she was a thousand times

19

more intelligent, more precious, more perceptive than all of them put together – these people who dared to bring her up, to teach her? These unsophisticated, crass nouveaux riches? She had been laughing at them all evening, but of course they hadn't even realised ... She could laugh or cry right under their noses and they wouldn't deign to notice ... To them a fourteen-year-old was just a kid – to be pushed around like a dog! What right did they have to send her to bed, to punish her, to insult her? 'Oh, I wish they were all dead,' she exclaimed. Through the wall she could hear the Englishwoman breathing softly as she slept. Antoinette started crying again, but more quietly this time, tasting the tears that ran down her cheeks into the corners of her mouth and on to her lips. Suddenly, a strange pleasure flooded through her; for the first time in her life she was crying like a true woman – silently, without scowling or hiccoughing. Later on, she would cry the same tears over love ... For a long time she listened to the sobs rising in her chest like the deep, low swell of the sea. Her mouth was moist with tears and tasted salty. She switched on the light and looked in the mirror with curiosity. Her eyes were swollen, her cheeks red and mottled. Like a little girl who's been beaten. She was ugly, ugly ... She started sobbing again.

'I want to die! Dear God, please make me die ... Dear God, sweet Holy Virgin, why did you make me their child? Punish them, I'm begging you ... Punish them just once, and after that, I'll gladly die.'

She stopped suddenly and said out loud, 'Of course it's all a joke. The good Lord and the Virgin Mary are just a joke, like the good parents you read about in books and all that stuff about the happiest time of your life ...'

The happiest time of your life, what a joke! She was biting her hands so hard that she could taste blood in her mouth. 'Happiest ... happiest ... I'd rather be dead and buried ...' she kept saying over and over again, furiously.

Day in, day out, doing the same things at the same times ... It was slavery, prison! Getting up, getting dressed ... Dull little dresses, heavy ankle-boots, ribbed stockings – all on purpose, on purpose so she'd look like a drudge, so that no one in the street would even glance at her, so that she'd be just some insignificant little girl walking by ... 'Fools! You'll never be young like me again, with skin as delicate as a flower, smooth, fresh, and lustrous eyelashes, and beautiful eyes – sometimes frightened, sometimes mischievous – which can entice, reject, desire ... Never, never again!' But the desire ... and these terrible feelings ... Why did she feel this shameful, desperate envy eating away at her heart every time she saw two lovers walking by at dusk, kissing as they passed and teetering slightly, as if they were intoxicated? Why feel the hatred of a spinster at only fourteen? She would have her share eventually, she knew that. But it was so far off, so very far it seemed it would never come ... and, in the meantime, this harsh life of humiliation, lessons, strict discipline, shouting from her mother ...

'The woman dared to threaten me!' she said out loud. 'She shouldn't have dared ...'

Then she remembered her mother's raised hand.

'If she had touched me, I would have scratched her, bitten her, and then ... But it's always possible to escape ... for ever ... There's the window,' she thought feverishly.

She imagined herself lying on the street, covered in blood. No ball on the fifteenth ... 'Couldn't the child have chosen another day to kill herself?' they'd say. As her mother had said, '*I* want to live, *I, I* ...' Perhaps, in the end, that's what hurt more than all the rest: never before had Antoinette seen in her mother's eyes that cold look, the look a woman would give to a rival.

'Dirty selfish pigs. *I'm* the one who wants to live, *me*! I'm young ... They're cheating me, they're stealing my share of happiness . . . Oh, if only, by some miracle, I could go to the ball! To be the most beautiful, the most dazzling woman there, with all the men at my feet!'

She lowered her voice to a whisper.

'Do you know who she is? That's Mademoiselle Kampf. She's not pretty in the conventional sense, you know, but she is extraordinarily charming . . . and so sophisticated. The others all pale by comparison, don't you agree? As for her mother, well, she looks like a kitchen maid compared to her daughter . . .'

She laid her head on the tear-soaked pillow and closed her eyes; her weary limbs were overcome by a feeling of soft, gentle sensuality. She tenderly touched her body through her nightdress with light, respectful fingers. A beautiful body, ready for love . . .

'Fifteen, O Romeo, that's how old Juliet was . . .' she murmured.

Once she was fifteen, it would all be different; then she would savour life . . .

4

Madame Kampf said nothing about the previous night's argument to Antoinette, but all through lunch she let her daughter know she was in a bad mood by barking out the kind of curt reprimands at which she excelled when she was angry.

'What are you daydreaming about with your mouth hanging open like that? Close it and breathe through your nose. How nice for parents to have a daughter who always has her head in the clouds! Will you pay attention to how you're eating? I bet you've stained the tablecloth . . . Can't you eat properly at your age? And don't look at me like that! You have to learn how to take criticism without making faces. Is it beneath you to answer? Cat got your tongue?

'That's it, here come the tears,' she continued, standing up and throwing down her napkin. 'Well, I'd rather leave the table than look at your stupid little face.'

She went out, slamming the door behind her, and leaving Antoinette and her governess staring at the abandoned place setting opposite them.

'Finish your dessert now,' Miss Betty whispered. 'You'll be late for your German lesson.'

Antoinette, her hands trembling, picked up a section of the orange she had just peeled. She always tried to eat slowly and calmly, so that the servant, standing motionless behind her chair, would think that she despised 'that woman' and her constant nit-picking; but, in spite of herself, big, shiny tears fell from her swollen eyes on to her dress.

A little later, Madame Kampf came into the study; she was holding the packet of invitations.

'You're going to your piano lesson after tea, aren't you, Antoinette? You can give Isabelle her invitation, and, Miss Betty, you can put the rest in the post.'

'Yes, Mrs Kampf.'

The post office was very crowded; Miss Betty looked at the clock.

'Oh, it's late! We don't have time . . . I'll come back during your lesson, dear,' she said looking away, her cheeks redder than usual. 'You don't . . . you don't mind, do you, dear?'

'No,' murmured Antoinette.

She said no more; but when Miss Betty left her in front of Mademoiselle Isabelle's apartment building, urging her to hurry up and go in, Antoinette waited a moment, hidden behind the large doors leading to the courtyard. She saw the Englishwoman hurrying towards a taxi that was waiting at the corner. The car passed very close to Antoinette, who stood on tiptoe and looked inside, simultaneously curious and frightened. But she saw nothing. She stayed where she was for a while, watching the taxi disappear into the distance.

'I'd suspected she had a lover! They're probably kissing right now, like they do in books. Will he say, "I love you"? And what about her? Is she his . . . mistress?'

Antoinette felt a sense of shame and disgust, mixed with a kind of vague suffering. To be free and alone with a man – how happy she must be! They'd be going to the woods, no doubt . . .

'How I wish Mother could see them,' she whispered, clenching her fists. 'Oh, I do! But no . . . People in love are always lucky! They're happy, they're together, they kiss . . .

24

The whole world is full of men and women who love each other . . . Why not me?'

She was swinging her school bag in front of her. She looked at it with hate, then sighed, turned slowly, and crossed the courtyard. She was late. She could already hear Mademoiselle Isabelle: 'Haven't you been taught that being on time is the most important obligation of a student towards her teachers, Antoinette?'

'She's stupid and old and ugly,' thought Antoinette in exasperation.

To her face, she reeled out, 'Hello, Mademoiselle, it's not my fault I'm late. It was Mother: she asked me to give you this . . .'

As she held out the envelope, an idea suddenly struck her.

'. . . and she asked if you could let me leave five minutes earlier than usual.'

That way she might be able to see Miss Betty coming back with her man.

But Mademoiselle Isabelle wasn't listening. She was reading Madame Kampf's invitation.

Antoinette saw the dry, dark skin of her pendulous cheeks suddenly flush red.

'What's this? A ball? Your mother is giving a ball?'

Mademoiselle Isabelle turned the invitation over, furtively brushing it against the back of her hand to see whether it was engraved or just printed. There was a difference of at least forty francs . . . As soon as she touched it, she knew it was engraved. She shrugged her shoulders angrily. Those Kampfs had always been insanely vain and extravagant! In the past, when Rosine had worked at the Banque de Paris (and, good God, it wasn't so very long ago), she'd spent all her wages on clothes. She wore silk lingerie, a different pair of gloves every week . . . But then again, she frequented, no doubt, the most disreputable places. It was only that kind of woman who found happiness. The others . . .

'Your mother has always been lucky,' she muttered bitterly.

'She's furious,' Antoinette said to herself. 'But you'll definitely be coming, won't you?' she asked with a malicious little smile.

'I'll let you know. I'll do my very best because I'd really like to see your mother,' said Mademoiselle Isabelle. 'But, on the other hand, I don't know if I can . . . Some friends – the parents of one of my younger students, Monsieur and Madame Aristide Gros, the former cabinet private secretary (I'm sure your father has heard of him) . . . I've known them for years – they've invited me to the theatre, and I've already accepted . . . But I'll see what I can do,' she added, without going into further detail. 'In any case, tell your mother that I would be delighted, just delighted to see her . . .'

'I will, Mademoiselle.'

'Now then, to work. Come along, sit down . . .'

Antoinette slowly adjusted the velour piano stool. She could have reproduced every stain, every rip in the material from memory. As she began her scales she stared mournfully at a yellow vase on the mantelpiece. It was full of dust inside, never a flower . . . And those hideous little shell boxes on the shelves. How ugly this dark little apartment was, how shabby and foreboding this place that, for years, she'd been forced to come to . . .

While Mademoiselle Isabelle arranged the sheet music, she cast a furtive look out of the window. (It must be very beautiful in the woods, at dusk, with the bare, delicate trees and the winter sky as white as a pearl . . .) Three times a week, every week, for six years! Would it go on until she died?

'Antoinette, Antoinette, where are you putting your hands? Start again, please . . . Will there be many people going to your mother's ball?'

'I think Mama has invited two hundred people.'

'Goodness! Does she think there will be enough room? Isn't she worried it will get terribly hot and crowded? Play louder, Antoinette, put some spirit into it. Your left hand is weak, my dear ... This scale for next time and exercise eighteen in the third Czerny book ...'

Scales, exercises ... for months and months: Grieg's *Death of Ase*, Mendelssohn's *Songs without Words*, the 'Barcarole' from the *Tales of Hoffmann* ... Beneath her schoolgirl's fingers they all disintegrated into a harsh din ...

Mademoiselle Isabelle banged out the beat with a rolled-up notebook.

'Why are you pressing the keys like that? *Staccato, staccato*! Do you think I can't see how you're holding your ring-finger and your little finger? Two hundred people, you say? Do you know them all?'

'No.'

'Will your mother be wearing that new pink dress from Premet?'

Antoinette didn't answer.

'And what about you? You'll be going to the ball, I imagine? You're old enough ...'

'I don't know,' whispered Antoinette with a shiver.

'Faster, faster! This is how it should go: one, two, one, two, one, two ... Come along, wake up, Antoinette! The next section, my dear ...'

The next section ... dotted with sharps to stumble over! In the next-door apartment a child was crying. Mademoiselle Isabelle switched on the lamp. Outside, the sky had grown dark ... The clock struck four. Another hour had flowed through her fingers like water – lost, never to return. She wanted to be far away, or to die ...

'Are you tired, Antoinette? Already? When I was your age, I used to practise for six hours a day. Now, wait a moment. Don't leave so fast – you're in such a hurry ... What time should I come on the fifteenth?'

'It says on the invitation. Ten o'clock.'

'Good. But I'll see you before then.'

'Yes, Mademoiselle.'

Outside, the street was empty. Antoinette huddled against the wall and waited. A moment later, she heard Miss Betty's footsteps, and saw her walking quickly towards her holding the arm of a young man. Antoinette lurched forward and bumped straight into the couple. Miss Betty let out a little cry.

'Miss Betty!' said Antoinette. 'I've been waiting for you for at least fifteen minutes . . .'

Miss Betty's face was right up against hers; in a flash, her features were so changed that Antoinette stopped short, as if not recognising the person she was talking to. But she failed to notice her pitiful little mouth, gaping open, as bruised as a ravaged flower; she was staring at the man.

He was very young. A university student – maybe even still at school. His fresh lips were slightly swollen from shaving; his lovely eyes were mischievous. He was smoking. While Miss Betty stammered excuses, he said calmly and boldly, 'Introduce me, cousin.'

'Ann-toinette, this is my cousin,' murmured Miss Betty.

Antoinette held out her hand. The boy gave a laugh, then said nothing; he seemed to think for a moment before suggesting, 'Let me walk you home, all right?'

The three of them went down the dark, empty street in silence. The cool wind brushed against Antoinette's face; it was damp from the rain, as if misty with tears. She slowed down, watching the lovers in front of her, their bodies pressed together, neither of them speaking. How quickly they walked . . . She stopped. They didn't even turn round. 'If I were hit by a car, would they even know?' she thought with bitterness. A man bumped into her as he passed by; she jumped back in fright. But it was only the lamplighter; she watched how each street-lamp burst into flame as he touched one after the other with his long stick. The lights shimmered and danced like candles in the wind . . . Suddenly, she felt afraid. She ran ahead as fast as she could.

She caught up with the lovers at the Alexandre III Bridge. They were standing close together, whispering to each other urgently. The boy looked impatient when he saw Antoinette. Miss Betty was flustered for a moment; then, struck by sudden inspiration, she opened her handbag and took out the packet of envelopes.

'Here, dear, take your mother's invitations. I haven't posted them yet. Run down to the little tobacconist's shop, over there, down that little street on the left . . . Can you see its light? You can put them in the letterbox. We'll wait for you here.'

She thrust the packet of invitations into Antoinette's hand; then she quickly walked away. Antoinette saw her stop in the middle of the bridge and lower her head as she waited for the boy. They leaned against the parapet.

Antoinette hadn't moved. Because of the darkness, she could see only two shapeless shadows and the dark Seine reflecting the shimmering lights. Even when they kissed, she imagined rather than saw them leaning towards each other, their faces almost melting together. She began wringing her hands like a jealous woman. One of the envelopes slipped from her fingers and fell to the ground . . . She was frightened and quickly picked it up, but then she felt ashamed she'd been afraid. Was she always going to tremble like a little girl? Well, was she? She wasn't worthy of being a woman. And what about those two who were still kissing? Their lips were still pressed together! A kind of giddiness took hold of her: the wild need to do something outrageous and evil. She clenched her teeth, crumpled up all the invitations, tore them into little pieces and threw them into the Seine. For a long while, her heart pounding, she watched them floating, caught against one of the bridge's arches. And then the wind finally swept them deep into the water.

5

It was nearly six o'clock and Antoinette was coming back from a walk with Miss Betty. As no one answered when they rang the bell, Miss Betty knocked. They could hear the sound of furniture being moved behind the door.

'They must be getting the cloakroom ready,' said the governess. 'The ball's tonight. I keep forgetting . . . and you, dear?'

She gave Antoinette a tender smile of complicity, but her face was anxious. She hadn't seen her young lover again in front of the girl, but ever since that encounter in the street, Antoinette had been so aloof that her silences, her looks, worried Miss Betty . . .

When the servant opened the door they were immediately greeted by a furious Madame Kampf, who was overseeing the electrician in the dining room.

'Couldn't you use the service entrance?' she shouted angrily. 'You can see very well that we're setting up a cloakroom here. Now we'll have to start all over again. We'll never get it done,' she concluded, grabbing hold of a table to help the concierge and Georges, who were setting up the room.

In the dining room and the long adjoining hallway, six waiters in white cotton jackets were preparing the tables for the supper. In the middle was the buffet, decorated with stunning flowers.

30

Antoinette wanted to go to her room; Madame Kampf again started shouting:

'Not that way, not that way ... Your room is to be the bar, and yours, Miss Betty, is being used as well. Miss Betty will sleep in the linen room tonight, and you, Antoinette, in the little boxroom ... It's at the other end of the apartment, so you'll be able to sleep. You won't even hear the music ... What are you doing?' she said to the electrician, who was working unhurriedly and humming to himself. 'Can't you see that this light bulb isn't working ...'

'Give it time, lady ...'

Rosine shrugged her shoulders, annoyed.

'Time!' she muttered to herself. 'Time! He's been at it for an hour ...'

She clenched her fists as she spoke, with a gesture so identical to the one Antoinette made when she was angry that the girl, motionless at the doorway, began to tremble – like someone who unexpectedly finds herself standing in front of a mirror.

Madame Kampf was wearing a silk dressing-gown and slippers on her bare feet; her loose hair hung like writhing snakes round her fiery face. She caught sight of the florist, his arms full of roses, trying to make his way past Antoinette, who was leaning against the wall.

'Excuse me, young lady ...'

'Get out of the way for goodness sake!' she screamed, so sharply that Antoinette lurched into the florist and knocked the petals off one of the roses with her elbow.

'You are unbearable,' Madame Kampf continued, shouting so loudly that the glassware on the table started to vibrate. 'Why are you here, getting in the way and bothering everyone? Get out, go on, go to your room – no, not to your room, to the linen room; go wherever you please but just get out of my sight! I don't want to see you or hear you.'

Once Antoinette had gone, Madame Kampf rushed

through the dining room and the butler's pantry – which was piled high with buckets of ice to chill the champagne – to her husband's office. Kampf was on the telephone.

'What are you doing?' she cried, the moment he'd hung up. 'You haven't even shaved!'

'At six o'clock? You must be crazy!'

'First of all, it's six thirty, and secondly, there might be a few last-minute errands to do; so it's best to be ready.'

'You're mad,' he repeated impatiently. 'We have servants for that . . .'

'Oh, it's just great when you start playing the aristocrat and gentleman!' she said with a shrug. '"*We have servants for that* . . ." Save your airs and graces for the guests.'

'Don't get yourself in a state,' Kampf replied, gritting his teeth.

'But how do you expect me . . .' cried Rosine, with tears in her voice, 'how do you expect me not to get in a state? It's all going wrong! The bloody servants will never be ready on time. I have to be everywhere at once, supervising everything, and I haven't slept in three nights. I'm at the end of my rope. I think I'm going mad!'

She grabbed a small silver ashtray and threw it on the floor; but this outburst seemed to calm her down. She smiled, slightly embarrassed.

'It's not my fault, Alfred . . .'

Kampf shook his head and said nothing. As Rosine was leaving, he called her back.

'Listen, I've been meaning to ask you . . . Have you still not received any replies to the invitations?'

'No, why?'

'I don't know, it just seems odd to me . . . As if there's something going on. I wanted to ask Barthélemy if he'd received his invitation, but I haven't seen him at the Stock Market for over a week . . . Should I telephone him?'

'Now? That would be ridiculous.'

'Still, it's very odd . . .' said Kampf.

'Well, people just don't bother replying, that's all!' interrupted his wife. 'You either go or you don't . . . And do you know what? It even makes me happy. It means that no one wanted to let us down. Otherwise they would have sent their apologies, don't you think?'

Since her husband didn't reply, she asked him again, impatiently, 'Well don't you agree, Alfred? I'm right, aren't I? What do you think?'

Kampf spread out his arms.

'I have no idea . . . What do you want me to say? I don't know any more than you do . . .'

They looked at each other for a moment in silence. Rosine sighed and lowered her head.

'Oh, my God! We're finished, aren't we?'

'It'll be all right,' said Kampf.

'I know, but in the meantime . . . Oh, if you knew how frightened I am! I wish it were over!'

'Don't get yourself upset,' Kampf said again, rather unconvincingly.

He was absent-mindedly turning his paper knife over and over in his hands.

'Above all, say as little as possible . . . Just use the old clichés: "So happy to see you! Do have something to eat! It's so warm! It's so cold . . ."'

'The introductions will be the worst,' said Rosine anxiously. 'Think about it! All these people I've only ever met once, whom I will barely recognise . . . and who don't know each other, who have nothing in common . . .'

'Oh for God's sake, you'll think of something. After all, everyone's been in our position. They all had to start somewhere.'

'Do you remember our little apartment on the Rue Favart?' Rosine asked suddenly. 'And how we hesitated before replacing the old, battered settee in the dining room? That was only four years ago, and now look . . .' she added, indicating the heavy gilt furniture all around them.

'Do you mean,' he asked, 'that in four years' time, we'll be receiving ambassadors and then we'll remember how we sat here tonight shaking with fear because a hundred or so pimps and old tarts were coming? Eh?'

She laughed and covered his mouth with her hand. 'Well, really, do be quiet!'

As she was leaving the room, she bumped into the maître d' who was coming to warn her that the pretzels hadn't arrived with the champagne; and that the barman thought there wouldn't be enough gin for the cocktails.

Rosine put her hands to her head.

'Wonderful, that's all I need!' she shouted, starting her tirade all over again. 'Couldn't you have told me before? Well, couldn't you? Where do you expect me to get gin at this time of night? Everything is closed . . . and the pretzels . . .'

'Send the driver, darling,' Kampf suggested.

'The driver's gone to get his dinner,' said Georges.

'Of course,' screamed Rosine, beside herself, 'of course he has! He doesn't give a damn . . .' She checked herself. 'He doesn't *care in the least* whether we need him or not. He's off having his dinner! And he's not the only one I'll be firing tomorrow,' she added, looking at Georges and sounding so furious that the manservant immediately pursed his long smooth lips.

'If Madame means me . . .' he began.

'No, no, my friend, don't be ridiculous . . .' said Rosine with a shrug. 'It just slipped out. You can see very well that I'm upset . . . Take a taxi and buy whatever we need at Nicolas. Give him some money, Alfred . . .'

She hurried off to her room, straightening the flowers as she went and berating the waiters.

'This tray of *petits fours* is in the wrong place . . . Lift the pheasant's tail higher! Where are the caviar sandwiches?

Don't put them out too soon: everyone will make a mad dash for them. And what about the *foie gras*? I bet they've forgotten the *foie gras*! If I don't do something myself . . .'

'We're just unwrapping it now, Madame,' said the maître d', looking at her with ill-concealed contempt.

'I must seem ridiculous,' Rosine thought suddenly, catching a glimpse of herself in the mirror with her purplish face, frightened eyes, trembling lips. But nevertheless – like an overtired child – she felt unable to stop the hysterics, no matter how hard she tried. She was utterly exhausted and on the verge of tears.

She went into her room.

Her maid was laying out her ball gown on the bed; it was silver lamé, decorated with heavy layers of pearls. Her shoes shone like jewels, her stockings were made of silk.

'Will Madame be wanting dinner now? We will serve it in here of course, so as not to disturb the tables . . .'

'I'm not hungry,' said Rosine angrily.

'As Madame wishes . . . But could I at least go and have my dinner now?' asked Lucie, gritting her teeth, for Madame Kampf had made her spend four hours re-stitching all the loose pearls on her dress. 'May I remind Madame that it is nearly eight o'clock and that we are people, not animals.'

'Go on then, off with you! Am I stopping you?' exclaimed Madame Kampf.

When she was alone, she threw herself down on the bed and closed her eyes. But the room was as cold as a cellar: they had shut off all the radiators in the apartment that morning. She got up and went over to the dressing table.

'I look such a fright . . .'

Carefully she began to apply her make-up; first a thick layer of face cream that she mixed in her hands, then the liquid rouge on her cheeks, the black mascara, the delicate little line to extend her eyelids towards her temples, the powder . . . She worked slowly, stopping every now and then to look more closely – passionately, anxiously devouring her face in the mirror, her expression both scornful and cunning. In a fit of pique she took hold of a single grey hair near her temple and pulled it out with exaggerated violence. How ironic life was. Oh, how lovely her face had been at twenty! Her cheeks so rosy! But she'd had darned stockings and patched underwear . . . And now – jewellery, gowns, but her first wrinkles too . . . all at the same time. My God, how you had to hurry up and live! Not leave it till too late to be attractive to men, to love . . . What good were money, elegant clothes, and beautiful cars if you didn't have a man in your life, a handsome young lover? A lover . . . how she had yearned for one. When she was still a poor girl she had gone with men who spoke to her of love, believed them just because they were well-dressed, with beautiful manicured hands . . . Boors, the lot of them! But she was still waiting . . . And now, this was her last chance, these final years before old age set in, true old age, impossible to fight, inevitable . . . She closed her eyes, imagined young lips, an eager, tender look, full of desire . . .

Hastily she threw off her silk robe, as if she were late for some lovers' tryst, and started dressing: she slipped on her stockings, her shoes, her gown, with the peculiar agility of women who have never in their life had a maid. Then the jewellery . . . She had a safe full of it. Kampf said it was the surest investment. She put on the double strand of pearls and all her rings; she covered both arms with bracelets made of enormous diamonds; then she pinned on a large brooch of sapphires, rubies, and emeralds. She sparkled and gleamed like a treasure trove. She took a few steps back, looked at herself with a joyous smile. Life was beginning at last, finally! Who knew? Perhaps tonight . . .

6

Antoinette and Miss Betty were finishing their dinner in the linen room; it had been served on an ironing board balanced across two chairs. Through the door they could hear the servants rushing about in the butler's pantry, and the sound of dishes clanking. Antoinette sat motionless, her hands tight round her knees. At nine o'clock, the governess looked at her watch.

'You have to go to bed right now, dear . . . You won't hear the music from your little room, so you should sleep well.'

When Antoinette did not reply, Miss Betty laughed and clapped her hands.

'Come along, Antoinette, wake up, what's the matter?'

She took her to the dingy little boxroom where a fold-out bed and two chairs had been hastily set up. Across the courtyard were the brightly lit windows of the reception room and dining room.

'You can watch the people dancing from here,' Miss Betty said jokingly. 'There are no shutters.'

After she left, Antoinette got up and pressed her face against the glass, partly in eagerness, partly in fear; a large section of wall was lit up by the golden light from the windows. Shadows passed back and forth behind the tulle curtains. The servants. Someone opened the bay-window, and Antoinette could clearly hear the sound of instruments being tuned at the end of the reception room. The musicians had already arrived. My God, it was after nine o'clock . . . All week long she had vaguely expected some catastrophe to wipe her from the face of the earth before anyone found out; but the evening had passed like any other. In a nearby apartment, the clock struck the half-hour. Thirty, forty-five minutes to go, then . . . Nothing, nothing would happen. Of course it wouldn't. The moment they had come home from their walk that evening, Madame Kampf had leapt at Miss Betty and demanded, in that furious tone of voice that always made nervous people immediately lose their heads, 'You did post the invitations, didn't you? You're quite sure you didn't lose any?' and Miss Betty had said, 'Yes, Mrs Kampf.' Surely *she* was the one responsible, she alone . . . And if Miss Betty were dismissed, well, too bad, it would serve her right, it would teach her a lesson.

'I don't give a damn,' Antoinette stammered. 'I don't give a damn,' biting her hands so hard that her young, sharp teeth made them bleed.

'And as for *her*, she can do what she likes to me, I'm not afraid, I don't give a damn!'

She looked out at the dark, deep courtyard below the window.

'I'll kill myself, and before I die, I'll say it's all because of *her*, and that will be the end of it,' she murmured. 'I'm not afraid of anything, I've already had my revenge . . .'

She went back to looking out of the window. Her breath was making the glass misty; angrily she wiped it and pressed her face against it once again. Finally, out of frustration, she threw open both sides of the window. The night was fine and cold. Now, with the piercing eyes of a fourteen-year-old, she could clearly see the chairs lined up along the wall, the musicians around the piano. She stood without moving for so long that she could no longer feel her cheeks or bare arms. For a moment, she almost convinced herself that nothing had happened, that the bridge, the dark water of the Seine, the torn-up invitations carried off by the wind had all been a dream, that the guests would miraculously appear and the ball begin. She heard the clock strike three quarters of an hour, then ten o'clock. Ten o'clock . . . She shuddered and slipped out of the room.

She walked towards the reception room, like an amateur assassin drawn back to the scene of the crime. In the corridor, two waiters, heads thrown back, were drinking champagne straight from the bottle. She went into the dining room. It was empty, waiting – the great table in the centre, with its Venetian-lace cloth and floral decorations, weighed down with game, fish in aspic, oysters on silver platters, and two identical pyramids of fruit. Pedestal tables with four or six place settings were scattered around the room, laid with dazzling crystal, fine porcelain, vermeil and silver. Looking back, Antoinette would never understand how she'd dared walk the entire length of that great room with its dazzling lights. At the door of the reception room, she hesitated for a moment, then noticed the large silk-upholstered settee in the adjoining antechamber. She dropped to her knees and crept between the back of the settee and the flowing curtains; there was just enough room for her if she hugged her knees to her chest, and, by leaning forward, she could see the reception room as if it were the stage of a theatre. She was trembling slightly, still frozen from her long vigil at the open window. At that moment, the apartment seemed silent, calm, asleep. The musicians were talking quietly. She could see a black man with brilliant white teeth, a woman in a silk dress, huge cymbals like at a fun fair, an enormous cello standing in the corner. The black man sighed, strumming a kind of guitar that gave off a low hum, like a moan.

'We start and finish later and later these days.'

The pianist said a few words that Antoinette couldn't hear but that made the others laugh. Then Monsieur and Madame Kampf came in.

When Antoinette saw them, she instinctively flinched, as if trying to disappear into the floor. She crushed herself against the wall, buried her mouth in the fold of her bent arm, but she could hear their footsteps getting closer. They were standing right next to her. Kampf sat down in an armchair opposite Antoinette. Rosine walked around the room for a moment. She switched on the wall lights near the fireplace, then switched them off again. She was sparkling with diamonds.

'Sit down,' Kampf said quietly. 'It's idiotic to get yourself in such a state . . .'

Antoinette, who had opened her eyes and leaned forward so that her cheek was touching the wooden back of the settee, could see her mother standing in front of her. She was struck by the expression on her imperious face, an expression she had never seen before: a kind of humility – a mixture of eagerness and terror . . .

'Alfred, do you think everything will be all right?' she asked in a voice as quavering and innocent as a little girl's.

Alfred had no time to answer, for the sound of the doorbell ringing suddenly echoed throughout the apartment.

Rosine clasped her hands.

'Oh my God, it's beginning!' she whispered as if she were describing an earthquake.

The two of them rushed towards the open door of the reception room.

A moment later, Antoinette saw them come back, one on either side of Mademoiselle Isabelle, who was talking very loudly. Her voice was different from the one she normally used: it was oddly high-pitched and sharp, and interrupted by occasional peals of laughter that lit up her remarks like little sparks.

'I'd forgotten all about her,' Antoinette thought in horror.

Madame Kampf, radiant now, continued talking. She had reverted to her self-satisfied, arrogant expression; she winked maliciously at her husband, secretly indicating Mademoiselle Isabelle's dress of yellow tulle and, round her long, dry neck, a feather boa that she flapped with both hands as if she were one of the ridiculous courtesans in a Molière play. A silver lorgnette hung from an orange velvet band round her wrist.

'Have you ever been in this room, Isabelle?'

'Well, no, it's very pretty. Who chose the furniture for you? Oh, look at these little vases, they're just delightful. So you still like the Japanese style, Rosine? *I'm* always standing up for it. Why just the other day, I was defending it to the Block-Lévys, the Salomons, do you know them? They were criticising it as looking fake and typically 'nouveau riche,' to use their expression. "Well say what you like, I think it's cheerful, lively, and then, the fact that it's less expensive than the Louis XV style, for example, is hardly a defect, quite the contrary . . ."'

'You couldn't be more wrong, Isabelle,' Rosine protested crossly. 'Chinese and Japanese antiques are fetching ridiculously high prices . . . This period vase decorated with birds, for example . . .'

'Rather late in the period . . .'

'My husband paid ten thousand francs for it at the Drouot Auction House . . . What am I saying? Twelve thousand, not ten thousand, isn't that right, Alfred? Oh, I scolded him! But not for long. I myself have a passion for seeking out little ornaments. I just adore it.'

'You'll have a glass of port, won't you, ladies?' interrupted Kampf, gesturing to the servant, who had just come in. 'Georges, bring us three glasses of Sandeman port and some sandwiches, caviar sandwiches . . .'

Mademoiselle Isabelle had walked away; with the help of her lorgnette she was examining a golden Buddha embroidered on a velvet cushion.

'Sandwiches!' Madame Kampf whispered quickly. 'Are

you mad? You're not going to ruin my beautiful table just for her! Georges, just bring some plain biscuits from the china tray, do you understand, from the china tray.'

'Yes, Madame.'

He came back a moment later with the tray and Baccarat decanter. The three of them drank in silence. Then Madame Kampf and Mademoiselle Isabelle sat down on the settee where Antoinette was hiding. By reaching out her hand, she could have touched her mother's silver slippers and her teacher's yellow satin court shoes. Kampf was pacing up and down, glancing furtively at the clock.

'So tell me, who will be coming tonight?' asked Mademoiselle Isabelle.

'Oh,' said Rosine, 'some charming people, and some old fogeys too, like the Marquise de San Palacio, whose invitation I'm returning. But she does enjoy coming here so . . . I saw her yesterday. She was meant to be going away but she said to me, "My dear, I have put off my trip to the Midi for a week because of your ball: everyone always has such a good time with you . . ."'

'Oh, so you've already given some balls?' Mademoiselle Isabelle asked, pursing her lips.

'No, no,' Madame Kampf hastened to reply, 'just some afternoon tea parties. I didn't invite you because I know how busy you are during the day . . .'

'Yes, I am. Actually, I'm considering giving some concerts next year . . .'

'Really? What an excellent idea!'

They fell silent. Mademoiselle Isabelle once again studied the walls of the room.

'It's charming, absolutely charming, such taste . . .'

Once again, silence. The two women coughed now and again. Rosine arranged her hair. Mademoiselle Isabelle carefully adjusted the skirt of her dress.

'Haven't we had beautiful weather these past few days?'

Kampf broke in. 'Well really, are we going to sit around with our arms folded all night? People do come so late! You did put ten o'clock on the invitations, didn't you, Rosine?'

'I see I'm very early . . .'

'Not at all, my dear, what an idea. It's a terrible habit, arriving so late, it's deplorable . . .'

'Why don't we have a dance,' said Kampf, clapping his hands cheerfully.

'Of course, what a very good idea! You may begin playing,' shouted Madame Kampf to the orchestra. 'A Charleston.'

'Do you know how to Charleston, Isabelle?'

'Well, yes, a bit, like everyone . . .'

'Well, you won't be short of partners. The Marquis d'Itcharra, for example, a nephew of the Spanish ambassador. He wins all the competitions in Deauville, doesn't he, Rosine? While we're waiting, let's open the ball.'

The two of them walked away from the settee, and the orchestra started playing in the empty drawing room. Antoinette saw Madame Kampf get up, rush to the window, and press her face – 'Her as well,' thought Antoinette – against the cold glass. The clock struck ten thirty.

'Good Lord, what are they doing?' whispered Madame Kampf impatiently. 'I wish that old bag would go to hell,' she added, almost loud enough to be heard, and then immediately gave a round of applause and and called out, laughing, 'Oh, how charming, just charming! I didn't know you could dance like that, Isabelle.'

'She dances like Josephine Baker,' Kampf replied from the other end of the drawing room.

When the dance was over, Kampf called out, 'Rosine, I'm taking Isabelle over to the bar, don't be jealous now!'

'What about you, my dear, won't you join us?'

'In a minute. I just have to have a word with the servants and I'll be with you . . .'

'I warn you, Rosine, I'm going to flirt with Isabelle all night.'

Madame Kampf found the strength to laugh and shake her finger at them; but she didn't say a word, and as soon as she was alone, she once again threw herself against the window. She could hear the sound of cars in the street below. When some of them slowed down in front of the building, Madame Kampf leaned out of the window and strained to look down into the dark winter street. But then the cars drove off, the sound of their engines growing fainter as they disappeared into the night. The later it got, however, the fewer cars there were, and many long minutes went by without a single sound coming from the street. It was as deserted as a country lane; there was only the noise of the nearby tramway, and the muted hooting of car horns, far away.

Rosine's teeth were chattering, as if she had a fever. Ten forty-five. Ten fifty. In the empty drawing room, a little clock struck the hour with a hurried little chime, like silvery bells; the one in the dining room gave an insistent reply, and from the other side of the street, the bell of a large clock on the front of a church rang slowly and solemnly, growing louder and louder as it marked the time that had passed.

'Nine, ten, eleven . . .' cried Madame Kampf in despair, raising her diamond-covered arms to heaven. 'What's wrong? What's happened, dear sweet Jesus?'

Alfred came back with Isabelle; the three of them looked at each other without speaking.

Madame Kampf laughed nervously. 'This is rather strange, isn't it? Unless something's happened . . .'

'Oh, my poor dear, perhaps there's been an earthquake,' said Mademoiselle Isabelle triumphantly.

But Madame Kampf was not prepared to give up just yet.

'Oh, it doesn't mean a thing. Just imagine that the other day, I was at the house of my friend, the Countess

Brunelleschi: the first guests didn't start arriving until nearly midnight. So . . .'

Madame Kampf fiddled with her pearls. Her voice was full of anguish.

'It's very annoying for the lady of the house, very upsetting,' Mademoiselle Isabelle murmured softly.

'Oh, it's . . . it's just one of those things you have to get used to, isn't it?'

At that moment, the doorbell rang. Alfred and Rosine rushed to the doorway.

'Start playing,' Rosine called out to the musicians.

They started playing a lively blues number. No one came in. Rosine could stand it no longer.

'Georges, Georges, someone rang the bell, didn't you hear it?'

'It was the ice cream being delivered from Rey's.'

Madame Kampf couldn't contain herself.

'But I'm telling you, something terrible must have happened, an accident, a misunderstanding, a mistake in the date or the time, I don't know, something! Ten past eleven, it's ten past eleven,' she said again in despair.

'Ten past eleven, already?' exclaimed Mademoiselle Isabelle. 'So it is, but how right you are, time passes so quickly when you entertain, my compliments . . . Why, I do believe it's a quarter past, can you hear the chimes?'

'Well, it won't be long now before people start arriving!' said Kampf loudly.

They all sat down again; no one said another word. They could hear the servants in fits of laughter in the butler's pantry.

'Go and tell them to be quiet, Alfred,' Rosine said finally, her voice shaking with fury. 'Go on!'

At eleven thirty, the pianist came in.

'Do you want us to wait a while longer, Madame?'

'No, just go away, all of you, just go!' Rosine roared. She

seemed on the verge of a breakdown. 'We'll pay you and then just go away! There won't be any ball, there won't be anything at all. It's an insult, a slap in the face, a plot by our enemies to humiliate us, to kill me! If anyone comes now, I won't see them, do you understand?' she continued, more and more violently. 'You are to say that I'm not at home, that someone in the house is very ill, or dead, say whatever you like!'

'There, there, my dear,' Mademoiselle Isabelle hastened to say, 'it isn't completely hopeless. Don't upset yourself like this, you'll make yourself ill . . . Of course, I understand how you must feel, my dear, my poor darling. But people can be so cruel, alas . . . You should say something to her, Alfred, look after her, console her . . .'

'What a farce!' Kampf hissed through clenched teeth, his face ashen. 'Will you just shut up!'

'Now, now, Alfred, don't shout, you should be cuddling her . . .'

'Well, if she insists on making herself look ridiculous . . .'

He turned sharply on his heels and called out to the musicians, 'What are you still doing here? How much do we owe you? Now get the hell out of here, for God's sake . . .'

Mademoiselle Isabelle slowly picked up her feather boa, her lorgnette, her handbag.

'It would be better if I left, Alfred, unless I can be of some help in any way, my poor dear . . .'

As he did not reply, she leant forward and kissed Rosine on the forehead, who remained motionless, her eyes dry and unblinking.

'Good-bye, my dear, please believe how sorry I am; I do feel for you,' she whispered mechanically, as if she were at a funeral. 'No, Alfred, no, don't bother seeing me out; I'm going, I'm leaving, I'm already gone. Cry as much as you like, my poor Rosine, you'll feel better,' she called out again at the top of her voice from the empty reception room.

As she walked through the dining room, Alfred and Rosine could hear her say to the servants, 'Be careful not to make any noise. Madame is very upset, very distressed.'

Then, finally, there was the hum of the lift and the dull thud of the doors in the courtyard opening and closing again.

'Horrible old bitch,' murmured Kampf. 'If at least . . .'

He stopped short. Rosine suddenly leapt to her feet, her face wet with tears, and shook her fist at him.

'It's all because of you,' she shouted. 'It's all your fault, you fool! You and your filthy vanity, wanting to show off . . . It's all because of you! The gentleman wishes to give a ball! To play host! What a farce! Do you think people don't know who you are, where you come from? *Nouveau riche*! They really screwed you, didn't they, your friends, your so-called friends. Thieves, crooks, the lot of them!'

'And what about yours? Your counts, your marquises, your pimps!'

They continued to shout at each other, a surge of angry, heated words that poured out like a flood. Then Kampf said more quietly, through clenched teeth, 'When I picked you up out of the gutter, you'd already been around . . . God knows where! You think I was blind, that I didn't know? But I thought you were pretty and intelligent – that if one day I got rich, you'd make me proud of you . . . Well, I've been lucky, haven't I! Look where it's landed me: you've got the manners of a fishwife. You're nothing but an old woman with the manners of a fishwife!'

'Other men were happy with me . . .'

'I'm sure they were. But don't give me any details. You'll regret it tomorrow if you do . . .'

'Tomorrow? And what makes you think I'd spend another minute with you after the way you've spoken to me? You brute!'

'Leave then! Go to hell!'

He walked out, slamming the door.

47

'Alfred, come back!' Rosine called after him.

She waited, breathless, her face turned towards the reception room, but he was already long gone . . . He was taking the stairs. She could hear his furious voice in the street shouting, 'Taxi, taxi . . .' then it grew fainter, disappearing round the corner.

The servants had gone upstairs, banging the doors and leaving all the lights on. Rosine, in her dazzling dress and pearls, collapsed into an armchair and sat there, motionless.

Suddenly she made a violent movement that was so abrupt and unexpected that Antoinette jumped and banged her head against the wall. Trembling, she made herself as small as she could; but her mother hadn't heard anything. She was pulling off her bracelets one by one and throwing them on to the floor. One of the bracelets was heavy and beautiful, decorated with enormous diamonds; it rolled under the settee and landed at Antoinette's feet. Antoinette, frozen to the spot, just stared.

She saw her mother's face – the tears streaming down her cheeks, streaking her make-up. It was a wrinkled face, a face so distorted and scarlet, it looked childish, comical, pitiful . . . But Antoinette felt no pity; she felt nothing but a kind of contempt, a scornful indifference. One day, she would say to some young man, 'Oh, I was a horrible little girl, you know. Why once I even . . .' Suddenly, she felt blessed because her future was full of promise, because she had all the strength of youth, because she was able to think, 'How could anyone cry like that, just because of something like this . . . What about love, what about death? She's going to die one day. Has she forgotten about that?'

So, grown-ups also suffered over trivial things, did they? And she, Antoinette, had been afraid of them, had trembled because of their shouting, their anger, their vain, absurd threats . . . Ever so quietly, she slipped out of her hiding place. For a moment longer, still hidden in the shadows, she looked at her mother: she had stopped sobbing but remained huddled over, letting the tears flow down to her mouth without bothering to wipe them away. Then Antoinette stood up.

'Mother.'

Madame Kampf leapt out of her chair.

'What are you doing here?' she shouted nervously. 'Get out, get out at once! Leave me the hell alone! I can't even have a moment's peace in my own house any more!'

Antoinette, her face pale, stayed where she was, her head lowered. The shrill voice was still ringing in her ears, but it was distant and stripped of all its force, like the sound of false thunder in the theatre. One day, and soon, she would say to some young man, 'Mother will make a fuss, but never mind . . .'

Slowly she stretched out her hand and began gently stroking her mother's hair with trembling fingers.

'Poor mama, never mind . . .'

For a while, Rosine automatically continued to protest, pushing her away and shaking her contorted features. 'Go away, I tell you. Leave me alone . . .'

Then a weak, defeated expression came over her face.

'Oh, my poor darling, my poor little Antoinette . . . You're so very lucky – yes, you really are – not to have yet seen how underhanded, how malicious, how unfair people can be . . . All those people who smiled at me, sent me invitations . . . They were just laughing at me behind my back! They despised me because I wasn't one of them. Nasty bitches . . . But you wouldn't understand, my poor darling. And your father! Oh, you're all I have! You're all I have, my poor darling . . .'

She threw her arms round her. Since Antoinette's silent face was pressed against her pearls, she couldn't see that her daughter was smiling.

'You're a good girl, Antoinette . . .' she said.

LE BAL

It was at this moment, this fleeting moment that their paths crossed 'on life's journey'. One of them was about to ascend, and the other to plunge downwards into darkness. But neither of them realised it.

'Poor mama,' Antoinette said softly. 'Poor mama . . .'

Snow in Autumn

Translator's Note

Snow in Autumn was originally published under the title *Les Mouches d'automne* in 1931 by Éditions Bernard Grasset. The French title – which translates literally as 'Flies in Autumn' – refers to a passage in the novella regarding the immigrants who had come to seek refuge in Paris after the Russian Revolution:

> *Back and forth they went, between their four walls, silently, like flies in autumn, after the heat and light of summer had gone, barely able to fly, weary and angry, buzzing around the windows, trailing their broken wings behind them.*

In this novella, the term *Barine* is used, which was a name given in Russia to a member of the aristocracy; it roughly translates as *Master*, and *Barinia*, its feminine form, as *Mistress*. Since the term *peasants* has peculiar connotations in English, I have chosen to translate the French *paysans* as *serfs*, especially as this concept was particular to Russia before the Revolution. Where Némirovsky talks about *Les Rouges*, I have translated *Bolsheviks*; *Les Blancs* are the *White Russians*.

The Russian language has a unique system of diminutives or 'nicknames'. To help the reader, we have listed below the names of the main characters along with their variations:

Alexandre Kirilovitch Karine (deceased) = father of Nicolas Alexandrovitch

Nicolas Alexandrovitch = Kolinka = Kolia = father of Cyrille, Youri, Loulou, André

Hélène Vassilievna = Nelly = wife of Nicolas and mother of Cyrille, Youri, Loulou; (née the Countess Eletzkaïa)

Cyrille Nicolaévitch = Cyrille = Kirilouchka

Youri Nicolaévitch = Youri = Yourotchka

Loulou = Lulitchka

Tatiana Ivanovna = Nianiouchka = Tatianouchka = Niania (the faithful servant and main protagonist)

This early work by the author of *Suite Française* is a beautifully observed description of a family, and society, in crisis, and reveals Némirovsky as a worthy successor to Flaubert and de Maupassant.

Sandra Smith
Robinson College
Cambridge
April 2006

1

She nodded. 'So we say good-bye, Yourotchka . . . Take good care of yourself, my darling boy,' she said, as she had so often in the past.

How quickly time passed . . . When he was a child, leaving for school in Moscow in the autumn, he would come to say good-bye to her like this, in the very same room. That had been ten, twelve years ago.

She looked at his officer's uniform almost with surprise, a kind of sorrowful pride.

'Ah, Yourotchka, my boy, it seems like it was just yesterday.'

She fell silent, gesturing wearily. She had been with the Karine family for fifty-one years. She was the nanny to Nicolas Alexandrovitch, Youri's father; after him, she had brought up his brothers and sisters, his children. She still remembered Alexandre Kirilovitch, killed in 1877 at thirty-nine in the war with Turkey. And now it was the children's turn: Cyrille, Youri, it was their turn to go off to war . . .

She sighed, making the sign of the cross over Youri.

'Go, and may God protect you, my darling boy.'

'Of course, my dear.'

He smiled, a resigned, mocking look on his face. He had the heavy, youthful features of a serf. He didn't look like the other Karines. He took the old woman's small hands in his own; they were as hard as bark, almost black. When he started to raise them to his lips, she blushed and quickly pulled them away.

'Are you mad? You don't think I'm some beautiful young lady, do you? Go on now, Yourotchka, go downstairs . . . They're still dancing down there.'

'Good-bye, Nianiouchka, Tatiana Ivanovna,' he said, sounding a bit lazy and slightly ironic. 'Good-bye. I'll bring you back a silk shawl from Berlin, though I'd be surprised if I ended up there; but, in the meantime, I'll send you some nice fabric from Moscow as a New Year's present.'

She forced herself to smile, pinching her lips even more; they had remained delicate, but were now tighter and pulled inwards, as if sucked into her mouth by her ageing jaw. She was seventy years old, very small and fragile-looking, with a smiling, lively face; her eyes were still piercing at times, and at others, calm and weary. She shook her head.

'You make many promises, and your brother's just the same. But you'll forget us once you're gone. Well, may it be God's will that it all ends soon, and that you'll both come back home. Do you think this wretched war will soon be over?'

'Definitely. It will end quickly and badly.'

'You mustn't joke like that,' she said crossly. 'Everything is in the hands of God.'

She walked away, kneeling down in front of the open trunk.

'You can tell Platochka and Piotre to come up and take whatever they want. Everything is ready. The fur coats are on the bottom with the tartan rugs. When are you leaving? It's midnight.'

'We'll be all right as long as we get to Moscow by morning. The train leaves tomorrow at eleven o'clock.'

She sighed, shaking her head in that familiar way.

'Ah, Lord Jesus, what a sad Christmas.'

Downstairs someone was playing a light, lively waltz on the piano; she could hear the dancers moving across the old wooden floors and the metallic sound of the men's boots.

Youri waved. 'Good-bye, I'm going downstairs, Nianiouchka.'

'Go, my dear.'

She was alone. 'The boots ... the things for the old overnight bag ...' she mumbled as she folded the clothing, 'they could still be useful at war ... Have I forgotten anything? The fur coats are at the bottom ...'

Thirty-nine years before, when Alexandre Kirilovitch had gone, she had packed his uniforms the very same way. Dear Lord, she remembered it well. The old chambermaid, Agafia, was still alive then ... She herself was young ... She closed her eyes, let out a deep sigh, clumsily got up.

'I'd really like to know where Platochka and Petka are, the scoundrels,' she grumbled. 'May God forgive me. Everyone's drunk today.' She picked up the shawl that had fallen on the floor, wrapped it round her head and face, went downstairs. The children's wing had been built in the old part of the house. It was beautiful, with fine architecture and a large Greek pediment decorated with columns; the grounds stretched all the way to the next village, Soukharevo. Tatiana Ivanovna hadn't lived anywhere else in fifty-one years. She alone knew every cupboard, all the cellars, and the dark, deserted rooms on the ground floor that, in the past, had been the grand reception rooms, home to many generations.

She walked quickly through the sitting room. Cyrille saw her, laughingly called out: 'Well, Tatiana Ivanovna. So your dear boys are leaving, are they?'

She frowned and smiled at the same time. 'Now, now, it won't do you any harm to rough it a little. Kirilouchka ...'

He and his sister Loulou had the beauty, the sparkling eyes, the contented and cruel features of the Karines before them. Loulou was waltzing in the arms of her younger cousin, Tchernichef, a schoolboy of fifteen. She was dazzling, with rosy cheeks, fiery red from the dancing; her thick, long black hair coiled round her small head, like a dark crown.

'Time,' mused Tatiana Ivanovna. 'Time . . . Ah, my God, you don't notice how quickly it goes, and then one day you realise that these little children are taller than you . . . Lulitchka, even she's become a young lady . . . My God, and it was only yesterday that I was telling her father: "Don't cry, Kolinka, you'll feel better soon, my treasure." He's an old man now.'

He was standing in front of her with Hélène Vassilievna. He saw her, started, whispered: 'Already, Tatianouchka? Are the horses ready?'

'Yes, it's time, Nicolas Alexandrovitch. I'll have the baggage put on the sleigh.'

He lowered his head, gently biting his wide, pale lips.

'My God, already? Very well. What can you do? Come on then, come on.'

He turned towards his wife, smiling faintly. '*Children will grow, and old people will fret*,' he said, his voice as weary and controlled as ever. 'Isn't that so, Nelly? Come along, my dear, I really think it's time now.'

They looked at each other without saying a word. She nervously threw her black lace scarf over her long, supple neck, the only part of her that had remained as beautiful as it had been in her youth, that and her green eyes that shimmered, like water.

'I'm coming with you, Tatiana.'

'What for?' said the old woman, shrugging her shoulders. 'You'll only get cold.'

'It doesn't matter,' she murmured impatiently.

Tatiana Ivanovna followed her in silence. They crossed an empty little room. In the past, Hélène Vassilievna was known as the Countess Eletzkaïa. On those summer nights, she would come to see Nicolas Karine, and they would walk through this little door to go into the sleeping house ... It was here that she would sometimes run into the old nanny, Tatiana, in the morning. She could still picture her, pressed against the wall to let her pass as she made the sign of the cross. That all seemed long gone and past, like an eerie dream. When Eletzki died, she'd married Karine. At the beginning, Tatiana Ivanovna's hostility had upset and annoyed her, and often ... She was young then. Now it was different. Now she took a kind of sad, ironic pleasure in watching the way the old woman looked at her, how she recoiled from her, how prudish she was, as if she was still that young adulteress running to meet her lover beneath the old lime trees ... That, at least, she retained from her youth.

'You didn't forget anything, did you?' she asked out loud.

'Well, no, Hélène Vassilievna.'

'There's so much snow. Have them put some more blankets on the sleigh.'

'Try not to worry.'

They pushed the terrace door open with great difficulty; it creaked beneath the weight of the snow. The icy-cold night was filled with the scent of frozen pine trees, and smoke, in the distance. Tatiana Ivanovna closed her shawl round her chin and ran out to the sleigh. She was still as straight and energetic as she had been in the past, when Cyrille and Youri were children and she would go to look for them at dusk. Hélène Vassilievna closed her eyes for a moment, picturing her two eldest sons, their faces, the games they played. Cyrille, her favourite. He was so handsome, so ... happy ... She feared more for him than for Youri. She loved them both passionately. But Cyrille ... Oh, it was a sin to think such things ... 'My God, protect them, save them, grant us the blessing of growing old, surrounded by all our children ... Hear me, Lord! Everything is in the hands of God,' Tatiana Ivanovna always said.

Tatiana Ivanovna climbed up the steps of the terrace, shaking off the snowflakes that clung to her lace shawl.

They went back into the sitting room. The piano was silent. The young people were standing in the middle of the room, quietly talking amongst themselves.

'It's time, my children,' said Hélène Vassilievna.

Cyrille motioned to her. 'All right, Mama, in a second . . . One more drink, gentlemen.'

They drank to the health of the emperor, the imperial family, the allies, the defeat of Germany. After each toast, they threw their champagne flutes to the floor, and the servants silently cleared away the broken glass. The rest of the servants were waiting in the entrance hall.

When the officers passed in front of them, they all spoke at exactly the same time, as if they were reciting a mournful lesson they had learned by heart: 'Well . . . Good-bye, Cyrille Nicolaévitch . . . Good-bye, Youri Nicolaévitch.' It was only Antipe, the old chef, always slightly tipsy and sad, who leaned his large grey head on his shoulder and added automatically in his loud, hoarse voice: 'May God keep you safe and sound.'

'Times have changed,' grumbled Tatiana Ivanovna. 'In the past, when the Barines left . . . Times have changed, and so have people.'

She followed Cyrille and Youri out on to the terrace. The snow was falling fast. The servants raised their lanterns, lighting up the ancient, frozen grounds, so still; and the statues at the foot of the drive, two Bellonas, goddesses of war who shimmered with frost and ice. One last time, Tatiana Ivanovna made the sign of the cross above the sleigh and the road; the young people called out to her, laughing as they leaned forward so she could kiss their cheeks, cheeks that were burning, whipped by the cold night air. 'There, there, my dear, good-bye, look after yourself, we'll be back, don't worry.' The driver took hold of the reins, made a strangely sharp whistlelike noise, and the horses started off.

One of the servants put his lantern down on the ground, yawning.

'Are you staying here, Nianiouchka?'

The old woman didn't reply. The others went inside. She saw the lights on the terrace and in the entrance hall going out, one by one. In the house, Nicolas Alexandrovitch absent-mindedly took a bottle of champagne from one of the servants.

'Why aren't you drinking?' he murmured, with difficulty. 'We should have a drink.'

Carefully, he filled their glasses; his hands were shaking slightly. A large man with a dyed moustache, General Siédof, went over to him. 'Try not to upset yourself, my friend,' he whispered in his ear. 'I spoke to His Highness. He'll look after them, don't worry.'

Nicolas Alexandrovitch slowly shrugged his shoulders. He had gone to St Petersburg as well. He'd been granted an audience and obtained letters. He had spoken to the grand duke. As if *he* could protect them from bullets, dysentery. 'Once your children have grown up, all you can do is fold your arms and let life run its course . . . But you still get upset, rush about, imagine . . . Yes, you do . . . I'm getting old,' he suddenly thought, 'old and cowardly. War? . . . My God, why twenty years ago I couldn't have imagined such luck.'

Out loud, he said: 'Thank you, Michel Mikaïlovitch. What can you do? They'll do what all the others do. May God grant us victory.'

'God willing!' the old general said passionately. The others, the young men who had been at the front, said nothing. One of them instinctively opened the piano, played a few notes.

'Dance, my dears,' said Nicolas Alexandrovitch.

He sat back down at the card-table, motioning to his wife. 'You should go and rest, Nelly. Look how pale you are.'

'So are you,' she whispered.

They silently squeezed each other's hand. Hélène Vassilievna left the room, and the elder Karine picked up the cards and started playing, fiddling absent-mindedly with the silver candelabra.

2

For quite a while, Tatiana Ivanovna listened to the sound of
the bells on the horse-drawn carriage growing fainter. 'They're
going quickly,' she thought. She had remained in the middle
of the path pressing her shawl tightly to her face. The snow,
light and delicate, felt like powder against her eyelids; the
moon had risen, and the deep trail left in the frozen ground
sparkled with a fiery blue glow. The wind dropped and
immediately the snow began falling heavily. The faint tinkle
of the little bells had died away; the pine trees, laden with
ice, creaked in the silence with the heavy groan of someone
in pain.

The old woman slowly made her way back to the house.
She thought of Cyrille, of Youri, with a kind of tender shock
. . . War. She vaguely imagined a field and galloping horses,
shells exploding like ripe pea pods . . . like a fleeting image
. . . where had she seen that before? In a schoolbook, no
doubt, one the children had coloured in. Which children?
Cyrille and Youri, or Nicolas Alexandrovitch and his
brothers? Sometimes, when she felt very weary, like tonight,
they became confused in her mind. A long, confusing dream.
Would she perhaps wake up, as she had in the past, to hear
Kolinka crying in his old bedroom?

Fifty-one years . . . Before, she too had a husband, a child
. . . They had died, both of them . . . It had happened so
long ago that sometimes she could barely remember what

they looked like. Yes, nothing lasted, everything was in the hands of God.

She went back upstairs to see André, the youngest Karine in her care. He still slept next to her, in the large corner room where Nicolas Alexandrovitch had slept, and then his brothers, his sisters. All of them had either died or gone to live far away. The room seemed too vast, the ceilings too high for the few pieces of furniture that remained: Tatiana Ivanovna's bed and André's, the white curtains and the little antique icon hanging over his cot. A toy chest, an old little wooden desk that had once been white but which the past forty years had worn so that it now looked a pale, glossy grey. Four bare windows, an old wooden floor. During the day, everything was bathed in a torrent of light and air. When night fell, with its eerie silence, Tatiana Ivanovna would say: 'There should be more children by now.'

She lit a candle, partially illuminating the ceiling's painted angels and their mischievous faces, then shaded the flame and walked over to André. He was in a deep sleep, his golden head nestled against the pillow; she stroked his forehead and his little hands that lay open over the sheets, then sat down next to him, as she always did. She would sit like this for hours, every night, half-asleep, knitting, drowsy from the heat given off by the wood-burning stove, dreaming of the past and the future: when Cyrille and Youri would get married, where new children would be sleeping there beside her. André would soon be gone. As soon as they were six, the boys went down to live on the floor below, with their tutors and governesses. But the old room had never remained empty for long. Cyrille? Or Youri? Or Loulou, perhaps? The burning candle crackled loudly, steadily, in the silence. She watched it, her hands slowly swaying, as if she were rocking a cradle. 'I'll live to see other children, God willing,' she whispered.

Someone knocked at the door. She stood up. 'Is that you, Nicolas Alexandrovitch?' she asked quietly.

'Yes, Nianioutchka.'

'Try not to make a noise or you'll wake him up . . .'

He came into the room; she took a chair and quietly put it next to the stove.

'Are you tired? Would you like some tea? It will only take a moment to boil some water.'

He stopped her. 'No. It's fine. I don't want anything.'

She picked her knitting up from the floor, sat down again, quickly clicking the shiny needles.

'It's been a long time since you came to see us.'

He said nothing, stretched his hands out towards the crackling wood-burning stove.

'Are you cold, Nicolas Alexandrovitch?'

He crossed his arms over his chest and shivered slightly. 'Have you caught a chill?' she cried, as she had in the past.

'No, not at all, my dear.'

She shook her head crossly and said nothing. Nicolas Alexandrovitch looked over at André's bed. 'Is he sleeping?'

'Yes. Do you want to see him?'

She stood up, took the candle and walked towards Nicolas Alexandrovitch. He didn't move. She leaned over, quickly tapped him on the shoulder. 'Nicolas Alexandrovitch . . . Kolinka . . .'

'Leave me be,' he murmured.

Silently, she looked away.

It was better to say nothing. And where could he cry freely, if not with her? Or Hélène Vassilievna . . . Yes, it was better to say nothing . . . She quietly retreated into the dark room. 'Wait here, I'm going to make some tea, it will warm us both up.'

When she got back, he seemed calmer; he was absent-mindedly turning the handle of the wood-burning stove; the plaster from the wall behind sounded like gently flowing sand.

'Look, Tatiana, how many times have I told you to plug

up the hole behind the stove. Look, look over there,' he said, pointing to a cockroach scuttling across the floor. 'They're coming from that hole. Do you think that's healthy in a child's bedroom?'

'You know very well that cockroaches are a sign of a wealthy household,' said Tatiana Ivanovna, shrugging her shoulders. 'Thank God, we've always had them here, and you were brought up here and others before you.' She handed him the glass of tea she had brought, stirred it. 'Drink it while it's hot. Is there enough sugar?'

He didn't reply, took a sip with a weary, distant look on his face and, suddenly, stood up.

'Well, good night, and get that hole behind the stove fixed, understand?'

'If you say so.'

'Bring the candle.'

She picked it up, lighting his way to the door; she went down the first three steps leading to the room. They were made of reddish brick – loose, wobbly, and slanting to one side, as if pulled towards the earth by a heavy weight.

'Be careful. Will you be able to sleep now?'

'To sleep ... I'm so sad, Tatiana, my soul is full of sadness.'

'God will protect them, Nicolas Alexandrovitch. People die in their beds, and God protects Christians from bullets.'

'I know, I know ...'

'You must trust in God.'

'I know,' he repeated. 'But it's not just that ...'

'What else is wrong, Barine?'

'Nothing's going right, Tatiana, it's hard to explain.'

She nodded.

'Yesterday, my great-nephew, the son of my niece in Soukharevo, was also conscripted for this cursed war. He's the only man in the family since his older brother was killed last spring. There's only his wife and a little girl the same age as our André ... so who's going to work the farm? Everyone has his share of misery.'

'Yes, we're living in sad times. I pray to God that ...'

He stopped her. 'Well, good night, Tatiana,' he said quickly.

'Good night, Nicolas Alexandrovitch.'

She stood silently, waiting until he had crossed the sitting room, listening to his footsteps creaking against the wooden floor. She opened the little window-pane. An icy wind was raging so fiercely that it swept up her shawl and blew through her hair. The old woman smiled, closed her eyes. She had been born in a region in northern Russia, far from where the Karines lived, and there was never enough ice, never enough wind as far as she was concerned. 'Where I come from,' she said, 'we used to break the ice with our bare feet, in the springtime, and I'd be happy to do it again.'

She closed the little window; the whistling of the wind was blocked out. The only sounds that remained were the faint rustling of the plaster trickling down the old walls, like whispering sand, and the hollow, deep creaking of rats gnawing away at the antique wooden panelling.

Tatiana Ivanovna went back into her bedroom, prayed for a long while, and then got undressed. It was late. She blew out the candle, sighed, and said, 'My God, my God,' out loud, over and over again into the silence, then fell asleep.

3

When Tatiana Ivanovna had closed all the doors of the empty house, she went up to the little cupola set into the roof. It was a hushed May night, already sweet-smelling and warm. Soukharevo was burning; she could clearly see the flames in the air and hear the sound of people's screaming carried through the wind from far away.

The Karine family had fled five months earlier, in January 1918. Since then, every day, Tatiana Ivanovna had watched fires burning in the distant villages, the flames die down and then flare up again, as the Bolsheviks took the villages from the White Russians who in turn lost them to the Bolsheviks. But the fires had never been as close as this evening; the flames lit up the abandoned grounds so clearly that she could see right down to the end of the long drive where the lilac trees had recently come into bloom. The birds, confused by the light, were flying to and fro as if it were daytime. Dogs were howling. Then the wind shifted, carrying away the sound and smell of the flames. The old, deserted grounds were calm and dark once more, and the perfume of the lilacs filled the air.

Tatiana Ivanovna waited a while, then sighed and went downstairs. In the downstairs rooms, they had taken down the carpets and draperies. The windows were boarded over and protected by iron bars. The family silver was hidden at the bottom of packing trunks, in the cellars; she'd buried the most valuable china in the old, deserted part of the orchard. Some of the serfs had helped her: they assumed that all this wealth would belong to them one day. These days, people cared about their neighbours only for their possessions. That's why they wouldn't say anything to the officials in Moscow, and later on, well, they'd wait and see ... Without them, though, she wouldn't have been able to do anything. She was all alone, the other servants had left long ago. Antipe, the cook, the last one left, had stayed with her until March, when he'd died. He had the key to the wine cellar and wanted nothing more. 'You're wrong not to have some wine, Tatiana,' he would say, 'it makes you forget all your troubles. Look, we're all alone, abandoned like dogs, and a curse on all the rest, I couldn't care less, just as long as I have some wine.'

But she had never liked drinking. One evening, during those final stormy March days, the two of them had been sitting in the kitchen. He'd started rambling, remembering back to when he was a soldier. 'They're not so stupid, these young people, with their revolution ... It's their turn now ... They've bled us enough, those bloody Barines, the dirty bastards.' She hadn't replied. What was the use? He had threatened to burn down the house, sell the jewellery and the hidden icons. He had carried on like this, deliriously, for a while, then, suddenly began to shout plaintively: 'Alexandre Kirilovitch, why have you abandoned us, Barine?' He'd started to vomit, a torrent of dark blood and alcohol poured from his mouth; he'd suffered until morning, then he'd died.

Tatiana Ivanovna fastened the iron chains on the sitting-room doors and went out on to the terrace through the little hidden door in the hallway. The statues were still in their wooden crates; they had been sealed away in September 1916 and left there, forgotten. She looked at the house; the delicate yellowish colour of the stonework was blackened by the thawing snow; beneath the acanthus leaves, the stucco was flaking off, revealing whitish marks, as if it had been struck by bullets. The windows in the greenhouse had been shattered by the wind. 'If Nicolas Alexandrovitch could see all this . . .'

She took a few steps down the path and stopped still, clutching her hands to her heart. There was a man standing in front of her. She looked at him for a moment without realising who it was, without recognising the pale, exhausted face beneath the soldier's cap. 'Is it you? Is it you, Yourotchka?' she finally asked, her voice shaking.

'Yes,' he said; the look on his face was cold, hesitant and strange. 'Will you hide me tonight?'

'Don't worry,' she said, as she had in the past. They went into the house, into the empty kitchen. She lit a candle, held it up to see Youri's face.

'How you've changed, good Lord! Are you ill?'

'I had typhus,' he said; his voice was slow, hoarse and husky. 'And I've been as sick as a dog, not far from here, in Temnaïa. But I was afraid to get word to you. There's a death warrant out for me,' he continued with the same steady, cold intonation. 'I need something to drink . . .'

She gave him some water and knelt down to loosen the dirty, blood-soaked rags tied round his bare feet.

'I've been walking for a long time,' he said.

She looked up. 'Why did you come? The serfs have all gone mad around here,' she said.

'Ah, it's the same everywhere. When I got out of prison, my parents had already left for Odessa. Where is there to go? People are fleeing everywhere, some to the north, others to the south . . .'

He shrugged his shoulders. 'It's the same everywhere . . .' he repeated apathetically.

'You were in prison?' she murmured, folding her hands.

'For six months.'

'But why?'

'Lord only knows.'

He fell silent, sat very still, continued with difficulty: 'I got out of Moscow ... One day, I found my way into a hospital train and the nurses hid me ... I still had some money left ... I travelled with them for ten days ... Then I started walking ... But I'd caught typhus fever. I collapsed in a field, near Temnaïa. Some people found me, took me in. I stayed with them for a while, but then the Bolsheviks were getting closer, so they were afraid, and I left.'

'Where is Cyrille?'

'He was in prison with me. But he managed to get out and join the family in Odessa; someone gave me a letter from him while I was in prison ... By the time I got out, they'd been gone for three weeks. I've never had any luck, my dear Nianiouchka,' he said, smiling in his usual way, resigned and ironic. 'Even in prison, Cyrille was in a cell with a beautiful young woman, a French actress, while I was locked up with some old Jew.'

He laughed, then stopped, as even he was surprised by the broken, hollow sound of his voice. He held her hand to his cheek. 'I'm so happy to be home, Nianiouchka,' he sighed, and suddenly fell asleep.

He slept for several hours; she didn't move, she just sat there opposite him, watching him; tears flowed silently down her ageing, pale face. A while later, she woke him up, took him to the nursery, put him to bed. He was slightly delirious. He was talking out loud, sometimes reaching out to touch the calendar on the wall, still decorated with a colour portrait of the tsar, or to grasp the rungs on the side of André's bed, where the icon was hanging, as if he were a child. He pointed to the page with the date: 18 May 1918, saying over and over again: 'I don't understand, I don't understand.'

Then he smiled as he looked at the window-shade billowing gently, and outside at the grounds, the trees lit up by the moon; and the spot, near the window, where the old wooden floor was slightly hollow. The pale moonlight washed over him, rocking him like a river of milk. How often had he got out of bed and sat right there, while his brother was asleep, listening to the coachman's accordion, the stifled laughter of the servants . . . He had inhaled the strong perfume of the lilacs, like tonight . . . He strained to listen, unconsciously trying to hear the music from the accordion in the silence. But he heard nothing except an occasional soft, low rumbling. He sat up, saw Tatiana Ivanovna sitting next to him in the dark room, tapped her on the shoulder.

'What's that noise?'

'I don't know. It started yesterday. Maybe it's thunder, you sometimes get thunder in May.'

'That?' he said. He laughed suddenly, staring at her with his wide eyes, eyes that looked pale but which burned with a feverish harsh light. 'That's cannon fire, my poor dear! I thought it would happen . . . It was too good to be true.'

His words were jumbled, confused, interspersed with laughter. Then he said quite clearly: 'If I could just die peacefully in this bed, I'm so tired . . .'

By morning, his fever had broken; he wanted to get up, go out into the grounds, breathe in the spring air, warm and pure, as in the past. Everything else had changed . . . The deserted grounds, full of wild grass, looked pitiful and sad. He went into the little pavilion, stretched out on the ground, absent-mindedly feeling the broken shards as he looked at the house through the shattered coloured glass in the window. One night, in prison, when he was expecting to be executed at any moment, he had seen the house in a dream, just as he did today, from the window of the little pavilion; but the house had been open, the terrace full of flowers. In his dream, he had seen every detail, right down to the chimney sweeps walking along the rooftop. He had woken up with a start and had thought: 'Tomorrow, I'll face death, that is certain. It is only just before dying that people have memories like this.'

Death. He wasn't afraid of it. But to leave this earth in

the turmoil of a revolution, forgotten by everyone, abandoned
... It was all so absurd ... Well, he hadn't died yet ...
Who knows? Perhaps he'd manage to escape. This house ...
He had truly thought he would never see it again, and here
it was, and these windows with their coloured glass that the
wind always shattered; he'd played with them as a child,
picturing in his mind the vineyards of Italy ... undoubtedly
because of their purplish colour, like red wine and blood.
Tatiana Ivanovna used to come in and say: 'Your mother's
calling you, my darling ...'

Tatiana Ivanovna came in carrying a plate with some
potatoes and bread.

'How have you managed to get any food?' he asked.

'At my age, you don't need much. I've always had enough
potatoes and in the village, you can sometimes get bread ...
I've never wanted for anything.'

She knelt down beside him, started feeding him, as if he
were too weak to lift the food and drink to his lips.

'Youri ... Don't you think you should leave right away?'

He frowned, looking at her without replying.

'You could walk to my nephew's house,' she said. 'He
wouldn't harm you: if you have some money, he could help
you find a horse and you could go to Odessa. Is it far?'

'Three or four days by train, ordinarily ... Now ... God
only knows ...'

'What can we do? God will help you. You could get to
your family and give them this. I've never wanted to trust
anyone else with it,' she said, lifting the hem of her dress.
'I have the big diamonds from your mother's necklace. Before
leaving, she told me to hide them. They couldn't take anything
with them, they left in the middle of the night when the
Bolsheviks took Temnaïa, and they were afraid of being
arrested. What kind of life must they have now?'

'Not a good one, I'm sure,' he said, wearily shrugging his
shoulders.

'Well, let's wait and see what happens tomorrow.'

'Look, you're kidding yourself, it's the same everywhere. At least here, the serfs know me, I've never done them any harm.'

'Who knows what they might secretly be thinking, those dogs?' she grumbled.

'Tomorrow, tomorrow,' he repeated, closing his eyes. 'We'll see what happens tomorrow. It's so peaceful here, my God.'

And so the day passed. Towards evening, he headed back to the house. It was a beautiful dusk, clear and peaceful, like the evening before. He took a detour to walk by the ornamental lake; in autumn, the bushes were bare, yet the lake was still covered in a thick layer of dead leaves, frozen beneath the ice. The flowers from the lilac trees fell like light rain; he could scarcely make out the dark water, faintly shimmering through, here and there.

He went back into the house, up to the nursery. Tatiana Ivanovna had set a table beside the open window; he recognised one of the little delicate tablecloths of fine linen reserved especially for the children when they were ill and ate in their bedroom; and the fork as well, the antique silver knife, the old tarnished cup.

'Eat, drink, my darling. I've taken a bottle of wine from the cellars for you, and I know you used to like potatoes baked in embers.'

'Not any more,' he said, laughing, 'but thank you anyway, my treasure.'

Night was falling. He lit a candle, setting it at the end of the table. Its flame burned tall and bright in the peaceful evening. It was so silent.

'Nianiouchka, why didn't you go with the family?' he asked.

'Well, someone had to stay and look after the house.'

'You think so?' he said, sounding sadly ironic. 'For whom, my God?'

They fell silent. 'Wouldn't you like to go and join them?' he asked.

'I'll go if they call for me. I'll find my way there; I've never been shy or stupid, thank God . . . But what would happen to the house?'

She stopped suddenly, whispered: 'Listen!'

Someone was downstairs, knocking at the door. They both stood up quickly.

'Hide, for the love of God, you have to hide, Youri!'

Youri went over to the window, cautiously looked outside. The moon was high. He recognised the boy who stood in the middle of the drive, stepping back to call out: 'Youri Nicolaévitch! It's me, Ignat!'

He was a young coachman who had been brought up in the Karine household. He and Youri had played together as children. He was the one who used to sing and play his accordion in the grounds on those summer nights. 'If *he* wants to hurt me,' Youri suddenly thought, 'then everything be damned, and me with it!' He leaned out of the window. 'Come up, my friend,' he shouted.

'I can't. The door is barricaded.'

'Go down and open the door, Niania, he's alone.'

'What have you done, you poor thing?' she whispered.

He made a weary gesture with his hand. 'Whatever happens, happens. And anyway, he saw me . . . Go on, my darling, go and let him in.'

She stood there motionless, trembling and silent. He walked towards the door. She stopped him, colour suddenly rushing back into her cheeks.

'What are you doing? It's not for you to go down to let in the coachman. Wait for me here.'

He gently shrugged his shoulders and sat down again. When she came back, followed by Ignat, he stood up and walked over to them.

'Hello, I'm happy to see you.'

'So am I, Youri Nicolaévitch,' said the boy, smiling. He had a big, full, rosy face.

'Have you had enough to eat?'

'God has helped me, Barine.'

'Do you still play the accordion, like you used to?'

'Sometimes.'

'I'd love to hear you play again . . . I'll be staying for a while.'

Ignat did not reply; he kept smiling, showing his wide, shiny teeth.

'Would you like a drink? Bring another glass, Tatiana.'

The old woman grudgingly obeyed. 'To your good health, Youri Nicolaévitch.' The young man drank.

They were silent. Tatiana Ivanovna walked over to them: 'Fine. Get going now. The young Barine is tired.'

'Even so, you must come with me to the village, Youri Nicolaévitch.'

'Ah! Why?' Youri murmured, involuntarily lowering his voice. 'Why, my friend?'

'You have to.'

Suddenly Tatiana Ivanovna looked as if she were about to pounce. An expression so wild, so strange, passed over her pale, impassive face that Youri shuddered.

'Leave him be,' he said almost despairingly to Tatiana. 'Calm down. I beg of you. Leave him be, it doesn't matter . . .'

She was screaming, wouldn't listen to him, her thin, tense hands stretched out like claws: 'Ah, you devil, you bloody bastard! You think I can't see what's in your eyes? And who do you think you are to be giving orders to your master?'

He turned towards her; his face had changed: his eyes were burning. Then he seemed to calm down, and said nonchalantly: 'Be quiet, old woman. There are some people in the village who want to talk to Youri Nicolaévitch, that's all.'

'Do you at least know what they want from me?' asked

Youri. He suddenly felt exhausted, one sincere, deep desire remained in his heart: to go to bed and sleep for a very long time.

'They want to talk to you about dividing up the wine. We've received orders from Moscow.'

'Ah! So that's it? I can see you enjoyed my wine. But you could have waited until tomorrow, you know.'

He walked towards the door, with Ignat following behind. At the doorway, he stopped. For an instant, Ignat seemed to hesitate; then, suddenly, with the same swift movement he used in the past to grab the whip, he reached into his belt, pulled out a revolver and fired two shots. The first hit Youri between the shoulders; he screamed in amazement, shuddering. The second bullet went right through his neck, killing him instantly.

4

One month after Youri's death, a cousin of the Karines came and spent a night with Tatiana Ivanovna. He was an old man, half dead from starvation and exhaustion, on his way from Odessa to Moscow to look for his wife, who had disappeared during the bombings in April. He brought her news of Nicolas Alexandrovitch and his family, and gave her their address. They were in good health, but were living in poverty. 'Could you find a man you trust,' he hesitated, 'to bring them what they left here?'

The old woman left for Odessa, carrying the jewellery in the hem of her skirt. For three months, she travelled along the roads, as she had done when she was young, when she made the pilgrimage from Kiev, sometimes climbing on to trains full of starving people making the journey south. One September evening, she arrived at the Karines' home. They would never forget the moment when she knocked at the door, when they first saw her, looking haggard and calm, her bundle of old clothes on her back, the diamonds beating against her weary legs. They would never forget her pale face, completely drained of blood, nor the sound of her voice when she told them that Youri was dead.

They were living in a dark room near the port; sacks of potatoes had been hung from the window-panes to absorb the exploding bullets. Hélène Vassilievna lay on an old mattress on the floor; Loulou and André were playing cards by the light of a little stove, where three pieces of coal were nearly burnt out. It was already cold, and the wind whistled through the broken windows. Cyrille was sleeping in one corner of the room, and Nicolas Alexandrovitch began what was later to become the main activity of his life: pacing back and forth between their four walls, hands folded behind his back, thinking about a time that would never return.

'Why did they kill him?' asked Loulou. 'Why, dear Lord, why?' Tears flowed down her face. She had changed, looked older.

'They were afraid he'd come back to claim his land. But they said he had always been a good Barine. They wanted to spare him the pain of a trial and execution, and that it was better to kill him that way . . .'

'The cowards,' Cyrille suddenly shouted. 'The bastards! Shooting him in the back! Bloody serfs . . . We should have been harder on you when we were your masters!' He shook his fist at the old woman with a kind of hatred. 'Do you hear me? Do you?'

'I hear you,' she replied, 'but what's the use regretting that he died one way as opposed to another? God has received him in his sacraments, I could see it in his peaceful face. May God grant all of us such a peaceful end. He saw nothing, he didn't suffer.'

'Ah! You don't understand.'

'It was better that way,' she repeated.

That was the last time she ever spoke Youri's name out loud; she seemed to have sealed her ageing lips over him, for ever. When anyone else talked about him, she never replied; she sat silent and cold, staring into space with a kind of icy despair.

The winter was extremely harsh. They didn't have enough bread or clothes. Only the jewellery that Tatiana Ivanovna had smuggled back occasionally brought them some money. The city was burning; the snow fell softly, hiding the scorched beams of the ruined houses, dead bodies, and dismembered horses. At times, the city was different: provisions arrived, meat, fruit, caviar . . . God alone knew how . . . The cannon fire would stop, and life would begin again, intoxicating and precarious.

Intoxicating . . . Cyrille and Loulou were the ones who felt it, the only ones. Much later, they would remember certain nights – going for boat rides with other young people, the taste of kisses, the dawn breeze blowing on the stormy waves of the Black Sea – and this would never fade in their memories.

The long winter passed, another summer and another winter followed, when the famine was so bad that dead children were buried in sacks, in mass graves. The Karines survived. In May, they managed to get passage on the last French boat leaving Odessa, first to Constantinople, then to Marseille.

They stepped out on the port in Marseille on 28 May 1920. In Constantinople, they had sold their remaining jewellery; their money was sewn into their belts, out of habit. They were dressed in rags, their faces were strange and frightening, miserable, harsh. The children, in spite of everything, seemed happy; they laughed with a kind of solemn gentleness which made the older members of the family sense their own weariness even more.

The clear May air was full of the scent of flowers and pepper; the crowd moved slowly, stopping to look in the shop windows, laughing and talking loudly. Lights and music echoed from the cafés, all of it as bizarre as in a dream.

While Nicolas Alexandrovitch went to find some hotel rooms, the children and Tatiana Ivanovna stayed outside for a while. Loulou closed her eyes, lifted up her pale face to breathe in the fragrant evening air. Great round electric lights lit up the street with a bluish glow; clusters of delicate trees in bloom swayed their branches. Some sailors passed by, laughed as they looked at the pretty young girl, standing motionless. One of them gently threw her a sprig of mimosa. Loulou started laughing. 'What a beautiful, charming place,' she said. 'It's like a dream, Nianiouchka, look . . .'

But the old woman had sat down on a bench and appeared to have dozed off, her headscarf pulled tightly round her white hair and her hands crossed over her knees. Loulou saw that her eyes were wide open, staring straight in front of her. She touched her shoulder, called: 'Nianiouchka, what's the matter?'

Tatiana Ivanovna suddenly shivered, stood up. At the same time, Nicolas Alexandrovitch waved to them.

They went inside and slowly crossed the entrance hall, feeling that everyone was looking at them oddly as they walked past. They were no longer used to thick carpets; they stuck to their shoes, like glue. An orchestra was playing in the restaurant. They stopped, listened to this jazz music for the very first time, with a vague sort of fear and mad delight. It was another world.

They went into their rooms and stood at the windows for a long time, watching the cars go by in the street below. 'Let's go out, let's go out,' the children said over and over. 'Let's go to a café, or the theatre . . .'

They had baths, brushed off their clothes, rushed to the door. Nicolas Alexandrovitch and his wife followed them more slowly, more hesitantly, but consumed as well, by a longing for fresh air and freedom.

When he reached the door, Nicolas Alexandrovitch turned round. Loulou had switched off the lights. They had forgotten Tatiana Ivanovna, who was sitting at the window. The light from a gas street-lamp in front of the little balcony lit up her bent head. She sat motionless, as if waiting for something. 'Are you coming with us, Nianiouchka?' asked Nicolas Alexandrovitch.

She didn't reply. 'Aren't you hungry?' She shook her head, then suddenly got up, nervously twisting the fringes of her shawl. 'Should I unpack the children's things? When will we be leaving?'

'But we've only just got here,' said Nicolas Alexandrovitch. 'Why do you want to go?'

'I don't know,' she murmured, a blank, weary look on her face. 'I just thought . . .'

She sighed, spread out her arms, then said quietly: 'It's all right.'

'Do you want to come with us?'

'No, thank you, Hélène Vassilievna,' she said with difficulty. 'No, really . . .'

They could hear the children running down the corridor. The adults looked at each other in silence, sighing; then Hélène Vassilievna made a weary gesture and went out, followed by Nicolas Alexandrovitch, who quietly closed the door.

5

The Karines arrived in Paris at the beginning of summer and rented a small furnished apartment on the Rue de l'Arc de Triomphe. It was a time when Paris had been invaded by the first wave of Russian immigrants, all of whom piled into Passy and the area around the Arc de Triomphe, instinctively drawn to the nearby woods of the Bois de Boulogne. That summer the heat was unbearable.

The apartment was small, dark, stifling; it smelled of dust and old upholstery. The low ceilings seemed to weigh down on them; from the windows, you could see the courtyard, long and narrow, with its whitewashed walls shimmering cruelly beneath the July sun. Even in the morning, they had to close the windows and shutters. The Karines remained in these four dark rooms until evening, without going out, stunned by the noise in Paris, feeling slightly sick as they breathed in the smells from the kitchens and sinks that rose up from the courtyard. Back and forth they went, between their four walls, silently, like flies in autumn after the heat and light of summer had gone, barely able to fly, weary and angry, buzzing around the windows, trailing their broken wings behind them.

Tatiana Ivanovna sat all day long in a small laundry room, at the back of the apartment, mending clothes. The only servant, a young girl from Normandy with a fresh face and rosy cheeks, as lumbering as a workhorse, would sometimes open the door and shout, 'Aren't you bored?' She thought the foreigner would understand her better if she spoke slowly and loudly, like when you speak to deaf people; her voice reverberated, making the china lampshade rattle.

Tatiana Ivanovna would vaguely shake her head, and the servant would go back to stirring her cooking.

André had been sent to boarding-school near the coast, in Brittany. A while later, Cyrille left. He had found his prison cellmate, the French actress he'd been locked up with in St Petersburg in 1918. She had a rich lover now. She was a pretty young blonde, generous, with a full, beautiful figure, and madly in love with Cyrille. It simplified his life. But sometimes, when he came home at dawn, he would look out of the window down at the courtyard, wishing he were stretched out on the pink paving stones, and finished, for ever, with all the complications of love and money.

Later, that feeling passed. He bought nice clothes. He drank. At the end of June, he went to Deauville with his mistress.

In Paris, when the heat broke towards evening, the Karines would go out to the Bois de Boulogne, to the Pavillon Dauphine. The adults would sit there, sadly listening to the orchestra playing, remembering the little islands and gardens in Moscow; Loulou, and the other young boys and girls, would walk along the shaded paths, reciting poetry, playing at being in love.

Loulou was twenty. She was no longer as beautiful as before; she was thin with angular movements like a boy, and rough, dark skin burned by the wind during their long sea crossing. On her face was a strange look, weary and cruel. She had so loved her active, dangerous, exciting life. Now, her very favourite thing was walking through Paris at dusk, and the long, silent evenings in the bistros, those popular little bars, with their smell of chalk and alcohol, and the sound of people playing billiards in the back room. Towards midnight, they would go back to one of their apartments and start drinking again, caressing each other in the darkened rooms. Everyone else was asleep; their parents only vaguely heard the sound of the gramophone playing until dawn. They saw nothing, or wanted to see nothing.

One night, Tatiana Ivanovna came out of her room to get some washing that was drying in the bathroom; she had to mend a pair of stockings for Loulou, and the night before, she'd left them on the radiator. She often worked at night. She didn't need much sleep, and by four or five o'clock in the morning, she was up, silently wandering through the apartment; she never went into the sitting room.

On that night, she had heard footsteps and voices in the entrance hall; the children had gone out ages ago, undoubtedly. She saw a faint light under the sitting-room door. 'They forgot to switch off the lamp, again,' she thought. She opened the door, and only then heard the gramophone playing, muffled by a pile of cushions; the low, breathless music sounded as if it were being played under water. The room was almost dark. Just one lamp, covered by a piece of red cloth, cast a shadow on the settee where Loulou was stretched out, apparently asleep, her blouse unbuttoned; in her arms was a young boy, his pale, delicate head thrown back. The old woman moved closer. They were actually asleep, their faces pressed against each other, their lips still touching. The smell of alcohol and thick smoke filled the room; all over the floor there were glasses, empty bottles, overflowing ashtrays, and cushions with the deep impressions made by their bodies.

Loulou woke up, stared at Tatiana Ivanovna, smiled; her dilated eyes, darkened by wine and passion, looked mockingly indifferent and extremely tired. 'What do you want?' she whispered.

Her long, loose hair reached down to the carpet; she tried to move her head, then groaned; the boy's hand was caught in her tangled hair. She broke free suddenly, sat up.

'What is it?' she said again, impatiently.

Tatiana Ivanovna looked at the boy. She knew him well; she had seen him often at the Karines' home when he was a child. He was called Prince Georges Andronikof; she remembered his long blond curls, his lace collars. 'Get him out of here, right now, do you hear me?' she said suddenly, gritting her teeth, her old face trembling and ashen.

Loulou shrugged her shoulders. 'All right, be quiet . . . He's going.'

'Lulitchka,' the old woman murmured.

'Yes, yes, just be quiet, for God's sake.'

She switched off the gramophone, lit a cigarette, put it out almost immediately. 'Help me,' she ordered curtly.

Silently, they tidied up the room, picking up cigarette butts and empty glasses. Loulou opened the shutters, greedily breathing in the cool air that wafted up from the cellars. 'Isn't it hot?'

The old woman didn't reply, looking away with a kind of furious modesty.

Loulou sat down on the window-ledge, gently swaying and humming. She looked sober, ill; beneath her face-powder, smudged from kissing, white patches of her pale cheeks showed through. She had rings under her wide empty eyes and she stared straight ahead.

'What's the matter with you, Nianiouchka? We do the same thing every night,' she finally said, her voice calm, hoarse from the wine and smoke. 'And in Odessa, my God? On the boat? You never noticed?'

'You should be ashamed,' murmured the old woman, sounding pained and disgusted. 'You should be ashamed! And with your parents asleep right next door . . .'

'So what? Oh, so that's it, are you crazy, Niania? We weren't doing anything wrong. We have a few drinks, a few kisses, why is that so wrong? Do you think my parents didn't do the same thing when they were young?'

'No, my girl.'

'Ah, so that's what you think, do you?'

'I was young once too, Lulitchka. It was a very long time ago, but I can still remember how my young blood burned through my body. Do you think anyone forgets that? And I remember your aunts when they were twenty, like you. It was in Karinova, in the spring ... Oh! What beautiful weather we had that year. Every day we would go for walks through the forest, take boat rides on the little lake ... And at night, there were always balls to go to, at home or at the neighbours' houses. Each young woman had someone they were in love with, and many times, they would all go out together, in the moonlight, in a troika. Your dead grandmother used to say: "When *we* were young ..." So what? They knew very well that certain things were allowed and others forbidden ... Sometimes, in the morning, they would come into my room and tell me all about what this one or that one had said. And still, they got engaged one day, got married, lived their lives honestly, with their fair share of happiness and sorrow, until the day when God took them. They died young, as you know, one in childbirth, and the other five years later after a nasty fever. Oh, yes, I can remember ... We had the most beautiful horses of all, and sometimes they would all ride out together, in a long line. Your father was a young man then; he and his friends, and your aunts, and some other young people, would ride into the forest, and the servants would carry the torches to light the way ahead ...'

'Yes,' said Loulou bitterly, pointing to the dingy little sitting room and the crude vodka that she was absent-mindedly swirling around at the bottom of her glass. 'The decor has obviously changed.'

'That's not all that's changed,' grumbled the old woman. She looked sadly at Loulou.

'Forgive me, my darling ... You shouldn't be ashamed,

I've known you since you were born. You haven't sinned, have you? You're still innocent?'

'Of course I am, my poor old dear,' said Loulou. She thought back to a night in Odessa, during the bombings, when she had slept in the home of Baron Rosenkranz, the former governor of the city; he was in prison and his son lived there, alone. The cannon fire had started so suddenly that she hadn't had time to get home, and she had spent the night in the empty palace, with Serge Rosenkranz. What had happened to him, to Serge? Dead, no doubt . . . Of typhus, starvation, a stray bullet, in prison . . . Take your pick. What a night that had been . . . The docks were in flames . . . They could see, from the bed where they were making love, walls of burning petrol engulfing the port . . .

She remembered the house, on the other side of the street, with its run-down façade and tulle curtains fluttering in the dark . . . That night . . . Death had come so close.

'Of course I am, Nianiouchka,' she repeated automatically.

But Tatiana Ivanovna knew her only too well: she shook her head, silently pursed her lips.

Georges Andronikof groaned, turned over clumsily, then half woke up. 'I'm utterly drunk,' he said quietly.

He stumbled over to an armchair, hid his face into its cushions, and sat motionless.

'He works all day in a garage now, and he's starving. If he couldn't drink . . . and enjoy other things, well, what would be the point of living?'

'You're offending God, Loulou.'

Suddenly the young girl hid her face in her hands and started sobbing violently.

'Nianiouchka . . . I want to go home! Home, home!' she kept saying, twisting her fingers in a strange and nervous way that the old woman had never seen before. 'Why have we been punished like this? We didn't do anything wrong!'

Tatiana Ivanovna gently stroked her dishevelled hair,

heavy with the odour of wine and smoke. 'It is God's holy will.'

'Oh, you do irritate me, that's your answer to everything!'

She dried her eyes, angrily shrugging her shoulders.

'Go away, leave me alone! Just go . . . I'm tired and upset. Don't say anything to my parents. What good would it do? You'd only upset them for nothing, and believe me, it wouldn't change anything. You're too old, you don't understand.'

6

One Sunday in August, when Cyrille came home, the Karines paid for a Mass to be said for Youri's soul. They walked together to the Rue Daru. It was a beautiful day; the blue sky was sparkling. There was an outdoor fair on the Avenue des Ternes, frenzied music and clouds of dust; the passers-by looked curiously at Tatiana Ivanovna, with her long skirt and her black shawl covering her head.

On the Rue Daru, Mass was celebrated in the crypt of the church; the candles crackled softly. You could hear burning wax dripping on the flagstones during the silences between the responses. 'May the soul of God's servant, Youri, rest in peace . . .' The priest, an old man with long trembling hands, spoke quietly, his voice sweet and muted. The Karines prayed in silence; they were no longer thinking of Youri, Youri was at peace, but for them, there was still such a long road to travel, a long, dark road. 'My God, protect me . . . My God, forgive me . . .' they said. But Tatiana Ivanovna, kneeling in front of the icon that burned faintly in the darkness, touched her head to the cold flagstones and thought only of Youri, prayed only for him, for his salvation and eternal rest.

Once Mass was over, they started for home. They bought some baby roses from a young girl they passed; she had dishevelled hair and looked cheerful. They were beginning to like this city and its people. Once the sun came out, you could forget all your troubles on these streets, you felt light-hearted without quite understanding why . . .

Sunday was the servant's day off. The cold meal was laid out on the table. They ate hardly anything, then Loulou put the roses in front of an old picture of Youri, when he was a child.

'He had such a strange expression,' said Loulou. 'I'd never noticed before . . . It's an almost indifferent, weary look.'

'I always saw the same look in pictures of people destined to die young or tragically,' murmured Cyrille uncomfortably, 'as if they somehow knew in advance and couldn't care less . . . Poor Youri, he was the best of all of us.'

They silently studied the little picture; it had faded. 'He's at peace now, free for ever.'

Loulou carefully arranged his flowers, lit two candles, placing one at each side of the picture, and they all stood motionless, forcing themselves to remember Youri. Now they felt only a kind of icy sadness, as if many long years had passed since his death. But it had been just two . . .

Hélène Vassilievna gently wiped the dust off the glass picture frame, without thinking, as if she were wiping tears from someone's face. Of all her children, Youri was the one she had understood the least, loved the least . . . 'He is with God,' she thought. 'He is happier than the others.'

They could hear the noise from the fair in the street.

'It's hot in here,' said Loulou.

Hélène Vassilievna turned round. 'Well, go out, my darlings, what can we do? Go and get some fresh air and look around the fair; when I was your age, I preferred the fairs in Moscow, on Palm Sunday, to the parties at court.'

'I liked them too,' said Loulou.

'Well, go on then,' their mother said again, sounding weary.

Loulou and Cyrille went out. Nicolas Alexandrovitch stood in front of the window, looking at the white walls, seeing nothing. Hélène Vassilievna sighed. How he had changed . . . He hadn't shaved . . . He was wearing an old waistcoat, covered in stains . . . How handsome and charming he had been, before . . . And what about her? She secretly glanced at herself in the mirror; her face was pale, her skin sickly and puffy, her flannel dressing-gown old and worn. She was old, an old woman, my God!

'Nianiouchka,' she said suddenly. She had never called her that. Tatiana Ivanovna, who was wandering silently between the furniture to tidy up wherever necessary, turned and looked at her with a strange, confused expression.

'Barinia?'

'We've grown old, my dear, haven't we? But you, you haven't changed at all. It makes me feel better to look at you . . . No, really, you're the same.'

'The only time people change at my age is in the coffin,' said Tatiana Ivanovna with a wry smile.

Hélène Vassilievna hesitated, then whispered softly, 'You remember what it was like at home, don't you?'

The old woman blushed suddenly, raising her trembling hands to heaven. 'Do I remember! My God! I could tell you where each and every thing was placed! I could walk through that house with my eyes shut! I remember every dress you ever wore, and the children's outfits, and the furniture, and the grounds, my God!'

'The sitting room with all the mirrors, my little pink sitting room . . .'

'The settee, where you used to sit on winter evenings, when the children were brought down.'

'And before that? Our wedding?'

'I can still see the dress you wore, the diamonds in your hair . . . The dress was made of moiré silk, and the antique lace from the late princess . . . Oh, my God, Lulitchka won't have anything to compare . . .'

They both fell silent. Nicolas Alexandrovitch was staring out at the sombre courtyard; he could picture his wife, the way she looked the first time he'd seen her, at the ball, when she was still the Countess Eletzkaïa, in her white satin evening gown, and her golden hair ... He had loved her so much ... They were still together at the end of their lives ... That was something. If only these women would stop talking ... If only he didn't have all these memories in his heart, life would be bearable.

'What's the point?' he said, gritting his teeth without turning round. 'What's the point? All that is over. We'll never get it back. Let other people hope if they want to ... It's over, over,' he repeated angrily.

Hélène Vassilievna took his hand, raising his pale fingers to her lips, as she had done so often in the past.

'Sometimes it all surges up from the depths of my soul ... But there's nothing we can do ... It's God's will ... Kolia ... My dear ... My beloved ... We're together, and as for the rest ...'

She made a vague gesture; they looked at each other in silence, trying to find other features, other smiles on their aged faces, from long ago.

The room was dark and hot. 'Why don't we take a taxi and go out tonight?' asked Hélène Vassilievna. 'Would you like that? There used to be a little restaurant, near Ville d'Avray, by the lake; we went there in 1908, do you remember?'

'Yes.'

'Maybe it's still there?'

'Maybe,' he said, shrugging his shoulders. 'We always assume that everything is being destroyed along with us, don't we? Let's go and see.'

They stood up and switched on the lights. Tatiana Ivanovna was standing in the middle of the room, muttering something they couldn't make out.

'Are you staying here, Nianiouchka?' Nicolas Alexandrovitch asked her automatically.

She seemed to wake up; her trembling lips moved for a long time as if she were having difficulty speaking.

'And where would I go?' she finally said.

When she was alone, she went and sat down in front of Youri's picture. She stared at it, but other images arose from her memory, from long ago, forgotten by everyone else. The faces of the dead, dresses from fifty years before, empty rooms . . . She remembered the first sharp, plaintive little cry Youri made when he was born. 'As if he knew what would happen to him,' she thought. 'The others didn't cry like that.'

Then she sat down in front of the window and started to mend the stockings.

7

During those first months in Paris, the Karines led a calm life. It was only in the autumn, when little André came back from Brittany, that they had to think about earning a living, as they were short of money. The last of the jewellery had been sold long ago. They had a little capital left, that might last two, maybe three years ... And then? Some Russians had opened restaurants, night clubs, small shops. The Karines, like many others, used their remaining money to buy and furnish a boutique, at the back of a courtyard. They began selling lace, icons, whatever remained of the antique china they'd managed to bring with them.

At first no one bought anything. In October they had to pay the rent. Then they had to send André to Nice. The air in Paris was giving him asthma attacks. They thought about moving. They were offered an apartment near the Porte de Versailles that was brighter and less expensive, but it had only three rooms and a kitchen as narrow as a cupboard. Where would they put poor old Tatiana? It was out of the question to make her climb up six flights of stairs, with her bad legs. Meanwhile, each month was becoming more difficult than the previous one. A succession of maids came and went, unable to get used to these foreigners who slept during the day and – at night – ate, drank, and left their dirty dishes everywhere in the sitting room, scattered about the furniture until the next morning.

Tatiana Ivanovna tried to do bits and pieces, like the laundry, but she was getting weak, and her old arms were no longer strong enough to turn the heavy French mattresses or lift the wet washing.

The children, constantly weary and irritable now, bullied her, chased her away: 'Leave it. Go away. You're getting everything mixed up. You ruin everything.' She would go without saying a word. Actually, she didn't seem even to hear them. She sat for hours on end, motionless, her hands on her knees, silently staring into space. She was hunched over, nearly doubled up; her skin was white, like a corpse, with swollen blue veins at the corners of her eyes. Often when she was called, she didn't reply, content with shutting her hollow little mouth even more tightly. She wasn't deaf, though. Every time any one of them said the name of a place, even if they spoke quietly, or whispered, she would shudder and suddenly say in a weak, low voice: 'Yes . . . on Easter Sunday, when the clock tower in Temnaïa burnt down, I remember that . . .' or 'The pavilion . . . after you'd gone, the wind had already blown out the windows . . . I wonder what's happened to it all . . .'

She would fall silent again and look out of the window at the white walls and the sky above the rooftops.

'When will winter finally come?' she would ask. 'My God, it's been so long since we had any cold weather or frost. Autumn is very long here . . . In Karinova, it's already all white, of course, and the river will be frozen over . . . Do you remember, Nicolas Alexandrovitch, when you were three or four years old, and I, even I was young, and your poor late mother would say, "Tatiana, you can tell you're from the north, my girl . . . The first time it snows, you go wild." Do you remember?'

'No,' murmured Nicolas Alexandrovitch wearily.

'Well, *I* remember,' she grumbled, 'and soon there won't be anyone but me who does.'

The Karines didn't reply. Each one of them had enough of their own memories, their own fears and sadness. One day Nicolas Alexandrovitch said, 'The winters here aren't like the ones at home.'

She shuddered. 'What do you mean, Nicolas Alexandrovitch?'

'You'll see soon enough,' he murmured.

She stared at him for a moment in silence. The haggard, defiant, strange look in her eyes struck him for the first time.

'What's wrong, my poor old dear?' he asked softly.

She didn't reply. What was the point?

Every day, she looked at the calendar that told her it was the beginning of October, then stared at the rooftops for a long time, but still there was no snow. All she saw were dingy tiles, the rain, the withered autumn leaves, carried along by the wind.

She was alone all day long now. Nicolas Alexandrovitch scoured the city for antiques or jewellery for their little shop; he managed to sell a few old things and buy some others.

In the past, Nicolas Alexandrovitch owned a collection of precious porcelain china and ornate silver platters. Now, as he walked home along the Champs-Elysées at dusk, carrying a package under his arm, he would sometimes manage to forget that he had to work for his family, for himself. He walked quickly, breathing in the smells of Paris, watching the lights shining at dusk, almost happy, his heart sad yet peaceful.

Loulou was working as a model in a fashion house. Ever so gradually, life took shape. They got home late, tired, returning home with a kind of excitement from the streets, from their work. It spilled over into discussions, laughter, for a while, but the solemn attitude of the silent old woman gradually wore them down. They would eat supper quickly, go to their rooms, and fall into a dreamless sleep, exhausted by their gruelling day.

8

October came and went, and the November rains began. From morning until night, they could hear the downpour pounding the cobblestones in the courtyard. In the apartment, the air was warm, heavy. When the heaters were switched off, at night, the humidity from outside seeped in through the grooves in the floors. The harsh wind howled behind the iron covers of the cold fireplace.

For hours on end, Tatiana Ivanovna sat in the empty apartment, in front of the window, watching the rain fall. Its heavy drops flowed down the glass like a river of tears. In all the kitchens, above the identical little pantries with their washing lines nailed up between the walls, where the dust cloths were hung to dry, the servants exchanged pleasantries, or complained, in this language they spoke so quickly that she couldn't understand a word. Around four o'clock, the children came home from school. She could hear the noise of pianos all being played at the same time; and, on each table, in the dining rooms, identical lamps were switched on. They pulled the curtains closed, and then she would hear only the sound of the rain and muffled noises from the street.

How could they all live like this, shut up in these dark houses? When would the snows come?

November passed, then the first weeks of December, barely any colder. There were heavy fogs, smoke coming out of the chimneys, the last dead leaves, crushed, carried along by the wind. Then Christmas. On 24 December, after a light meal, eaten quickly at one end of the table, the Karines left to celebrate Christmas Eve at the home of some friends. Tatiana Ivanovna helped them dress. When they said good-bye to her, she felt a spark of joy seeing them all dressed up, as in the past, Nicolas Alexandrovitch in a tuxedo. She smiled as she looked at Loulou in her white dress, her long hair in curls over her neck.

'Go on, Lulitchka, you'll meet your fiancé tonight, God willing.'

Loulou silently shrugged her shoulders, let herself be kissed without saying a word. They all left. André was spending the Christmas holidays in Paris. He was wearing the uniform from his school in Nice: a coat, short blue trousers, and cap; he looked taller and stronger. He had a quick, lively way of talking, the accent, gestures, and slang of a boy who'd been born and raised in France. That night he was going out in the evening with his parents for the first time. He was laughing, humming. Tatiana Ivanovna leaned out of the window, watched him walk ahead, jumping over the puddles. The heavy doors of the courtyard slammed shut with a dull thud. Once again Tatiana Ivanovna was alone. She sighed. The wind, mild for the time of year, full of fine raindrops, blew against her face. She raised her head, looked blankly up at the sky. Between the rooftops she could barely make out the shadowy horizon; it was coloured an extraordinary red, as if burning with an internal fire. In the apartment building, gramophones were playing on the different floors, merging to form a discordant music.

'At home,' Tatiana Ivanovna murmured, then fell silent. Why even think about it? That was over a long time ago . . . Everything was finished, dead.

She closed the window, went back into the apartment. She raised her head, breathed in the air with great effort, an irritated, worried look on her face. These low ceilings were suffocating her. Karinova ... The large house with its immense windows, where the light and air washed over the terraces, the sitting rooms, the entrance halls, where fifty musicians could fit comfortably when they held balls in the evenings. She recalled the Christmas when Cyrille and Youri had left ... She could almost hear the waltz they'd played that night ... Four years had passed ... She could picture the columns shimmering with ice in the moonlight. 'If I weren't so old,' she thought, 'I'd be happy to make the journey back ... But it wouldn't be the same. No, no,' she muttered vaguely. 'It wouldn't be the same.' The snow ... As soon as she saw the snow start to fall, she would be at peace ... She would forget everything. She would go to bed and close her eyes, for ever. 'Will I live to see the snow?' she whispered.

She automatically picked up the clothing from the chairs and started folding it. For some time now, she thought she could see a very even, fine sprinkling of dust that fell from the ceiling and settled everywhere. It had begun in autumn, when it got dark earlier but they lit the street-lamps later, to save on electricity. She brushed and shook the fabric endlessly; the dust flew off, but only fell back down again a bit further away, like a cloud of fine ash.

She picked up the clothing, brushed it off, muttering, 'What is this? What on earth is this?' with a painful, surprised look on her face.

Suddenly she stopped, looking around her. Sometimes she didn't understand why she was there, wandering through these narrow rooms. She placed her hands on her chest, sighed. The air was heavy, warm, and, unusually, the heaters were on, because it was a holiday; they gave off a smell of fresh paint. She wanted to switch them off, but she had never understood how to work them. She turned the little handle for a while in vain, then stopped. Once again she opened the window. The apartment on the other side of the courtyard was lit up and cast a rectangular swathe of bright light into the room.

'At home,' she thought, 'at home, at this time of year . . .' The forest would be frozen. She closed her eyes, pictured in extraordinary detail the deep snow, the fires in the village, shimmering in the distance; and the river and the grounds, sparkling and hard, like steel.

She stood motionless, leaning against the window-frame, pulling her shawl over her dishevelled hair, the way she always did. A fine, warm rain was falling; the bright raindrops, swept up in the sudden bursts of wind, wet her face. She shivered, pulled her old black shawl more tightly around her. Her ears were ringing; she felt as if a violent noise were beating through them, like a furious bell. Her head, her entire body, was aching.

She left the sitting room, made her way to her little room at the end of the hallway, and prepared for bed.

Before getting into bed, she knelt to say her prayers. She made the sign of the cross, then lowered her head to touch the wooden floor, as she did every night. But this evening her words were all confused; she stopped, stared at the little flame burning at the foot of the icon, almost in a trance.

She got into bed, closed her eyes. She couldn't fall asleep, so she just listened, in spite of herself, to the creaking furniture, the sound of the clock in the dining room, like a human sigh that announced the hour striking in the silence; and, above her, below her, the gramophones playing, this Christmas Eve. People were rushing up and down the stairs, crossing the courtyard, going out for the evening. She could hear people shouting constantly: 'Open the door, please!' the muffled echo of the courtyard door opening then closing again, and footsteps disappearing into the empty street. Taxis sped by. A hoarse voice called out to the concierge in the courtyard.

Tatiana Ivanovna sighed and turned her heavy head over to the other side of the pillow. She heard the bells chime eleven o'clock, then midnight. She fell asleep several times, woke up again. Every time she dozed off, she dreamed of the house in Karinova, but the image kept fading, so she hurried to close her eyes again to try to recapture it. Each time it happened, some detail disappeared. Sometimes, the delicate yellow of the stone changed into the reddish colour of dried blood; or the house was solid, walled over, the windows gone. But still she heard the faint echo of the frozen branches on the pine trees, whipped by the wind, like the sound of shattered glass.

Suddenly the dream changed. She saw herself standing in front of the open, empty house. It was in autumn, at the time of day when the servants lit the wood-burning stoves. She was standing downstairs, alone. In her dream, she saw the abandoned house, the bare rooms, just as she had left them, with the carpets rolled up against the walls. She went upstairs, and all the doors slammed in the wind, with a strange, groaning noise. She walked quickly, hurrying, as if she were afraid of being late for something. She saw all the enormous rooms, wide open, empty, with bits of wrapping paper and old newspapers scattered about the floor, swept up now and again, hovering in the wind.

Finally she entered the nursery. It was bare like all the other rooms, even André's bed was gone, and, in her dream, she felt a kind of astonishment: she remembered having rolled up his mattress and pushed it into a corner of the room herself. In front of the window, sitting on the floor, was Youri: in his soldier's uniform, pale and thin, just as he had been that last day, playing with some old jacks, like he had as a child. She knew he was dead, but still she felt such extraordinary joy at seeing him that her aged, weary heart began to beat violently, almost painfully; its deep, muffled rhythm pounded against her chest. She could see herself running towards him, crossing the dusty wooden floor that creaked beneath her weight, as it had in the past, but just as she was about to reach out and touch him, she woke up.

It was late. Day was breaking.

9

She woke with a moan and lay there motionless, stretched out on her back, staring at the bright windows, as if in a trance. A thick, white fog filled the courtyard; to her tired eyes, it looked like snow, like the first snows of autumn, thick and blinding, covering everything in a kind of mournful light, a harsh white glare.

She clasped her hands together. 'The first snow . . .' she whispered.

She looked at it for a long time, an expression of delight on her face that was both childlike and frightening, a little deranged. The apartment was silent. No one would be home yet, of course. She got out of bed and dressed without taking her eyes from the window, imagining the snow falling, ever faster, streaking the sky with a feathery trail. At one point, she thought she heard a door closing. Perhaps the Karines were already back and had gone to bed? But she wasn't thinking about them. She imagined she could feel the snowflakes on her face, could taste their fire and ice. She took her coat, quickly tied her scarf round her head and fastened it under her chin with a pin. Automatically she felt around on the table, looking for the keys that she always took with her in Karinova, when she went out, her hand stretched out as if she were blind. She found nothing, but kept feeling around anxiously, forgetting exactly what she was looking for, impatiently sweeping away her spectacle case, the knitting she had just started, the picture of Youri as a child . . .

She felt as if someone was waiting for her. A strange fever burned in her soul.

She opened the wardrobe, leaving its door and the drawer open. A clothes hanger fell to the floor. She hesitated for a moment, then shrugged her shoulders, as if she had no time to lose, and quickly left the room. She crossed the apartment and hurried silently down the stairs.

Once outside, she stopped. The freezing fog covered the courtyard in a dense, white blanket that slowly rose from the ground, like smoke. Fine drops of rain stung her face, like the tips of snowflakes when they fall amidst a September rain, half-melted.

Behind her, two men in tuxedos came out of the building and looked at her oddly. She followed them, slipping through the half-open door, which slammed shut behind her back with a dull thud.

She was in the street, a dark, deserted street; a gas-lamp shone through the rain. The fog was clearing and a cold sharp drizzle had started to fall. The cobblestones and walls shimmered faintly. A man passed by, his soaked shoes leaking water; a dog rushed across the road, came up to the old woman, and sniffed her, then followed her, whimpering and moaning miserably. It stayed with her for a while, then wandered off.

She kept walking, saw a square, other streets. A taxi drove past so close that it splattered mud on to her face. She didn't seem to notice. She walked straight ahead, stumbling over the wet cobblestones. Now and again, she felt so utterly exhausted that her legs seemed to give way under the weight of her body and sink into the ground. She looked up, saw day breaking near the Seine, a patch of white sky at the end of the street. To her eyes, it was a blanket of snow, just like in Soukharevo. She walked faster, dazzled by the fine, burning rain that stung her eyelids. The sound of church bells rang in her ears.

Suddenly she had a moment of lucidity; she clearly saw the smoke and fog as it lifted; but then the moment passed. She started walking again, weary and anxious, her body bent over towards the ground. Finally she reached the quayside.

The Seine was so high that it had overflowed its banks; the sun was rising, and the horizon was a pure, luminous white. The old woman walked over to the parapet and stared intently at the dazzling stretch of sky. Below her, a small staircase had been carved out of stone; she took hold of the hand-rail, clutched it tightly with her cold, shivering hand, and started down. Water flowed over the last few steps. She didn't notice. 'The river is frozen over,' she thought. 'It must be frozen over at this time of year.'

She thought that all she had to do was cross the river and on the other side would be Karinova. She could see the lights from its terraces shimmering through the snow.

But when she reached the last step, the smell of the water finally hit her. She made a sudden movement of surprise and anger, stopped for a moment, then continued descending, despite the water that soaked through her shoes and weighed down her skirt. And it was only when she was waist-deep in the Seine that she came back to her senses. She felt freezing cold and tried to cry out, but had only enough time to make the sign of the cross before her hand fell back.

She was dead.

Her little body floated for a moment, like a bundle of rags, before disappearing from sight, swallowed up by the shadowy Seine.